THE DRAGON PORTAL : PREQUEL

ESCAPE FROM FAERIE

JAMIE A. WATERS

Escape from Faerie © 2026 by Jamie A. Waters

Cover Art: Deranged Doctor Design
Editor: Tracy Dickey

ISBN: 978-1-949524-47-5 (Paperback Edition)
ISBN: 978-1-949524-46-8 (eBook Edition)

Library of Congress Control Number: 2025925215
First Edition *February 2026

Hidden Realms Publishing

THE DRAGON PORTAL SERIES

CHAPTER ONE

*L*iquid fire surged beneath Sabine's skin. The mental exercises she'd honed since childhood shattered beneath the agony searing through her left arm. She stared upward, refusing to betray her weakness by letting her tears fall.

"Good. Just a few more alterations," Elder Turvina murmured, clicking her tongue in approval. As one of the oldest fae in the Court, her magic carried enough weight to inspire a quiet deference from even the highest-ranking nobles. Not that it eased Sabine's resentment in that moment.

She pierced Sabine's skin again, sending a jagged pulse of magic through her nerve endings. The ink hissed faintly as the needle bit deeper. "Elegant, graceful, and powerful. This may be one of my best works yet."

As heir to the Unseelie throne, Sabine had been marked before—but never like this, and never with so much at stake. Sabine gritted her teeth, tempted to yank the needle from the woman's hand and stab her with it. A fresh wave of nausea rose, and her vision swam. Fighting to remain conscious, she struggled to breathe through the dense, cloying incense saturating the air. If she passed out, rumors would spread that she lacked the strength, will, and discipline necessary to acquire her marks. She couldn't risk shaming her lineage. The consequences were unfathomable—and deadly.

Sabine took a shaky breath, unsure how much longer she could last. Her silvery-white hair clung to her sweat-dampened skin, limp and tangled from the hours spent beneath Turvina's needle. The crystal hourglass had already been turned four times. Surely it couldn't go on much longer.

Turvina bent her head to study Sabine's arm and let out a pleased hum. The older woman's weathered, time-worn face was a rare sight among the fae. Most retained their youthful beauty for centuries, their features untouched by age until they ascended to Elderhood. Only those who had lived for over a thousand years, wielded immense magic, or endured great sacrifice bore the marks of time. Turvina had done all three. Despite the ancient burns covering her hands, her movements were steady and unhurried.

Sabine's gaze lingered on the painful scars marring Turvina's skin before she forced herself to look away. Most fae would have hidden such marks beneath layers of glamour, but Turvina wore them like the badges of honor they were. They served as a constant reminder of her sacrifice during the Dragon War. Turvina's parents and much of her family had been massacred while defending Faerie from foreign invaders, but she had survived.

Sabine remembered the whispered stories traded between the sidhe, how Turvina had once stood on top of the westernmost crystal tower, acting as an anchor for a binding ward meant to trap a greater dragon. When the beast unleashed its fire, they couldn't contain it completely.

Stepping outside the seal would have unraveled the magic, so Turvina had held her ground while the fae attacked. The flames scorched her flesh, but the ward held. The dragon was destroyed, and Turvina lived, changed and forever marked by the power she had wielded.

The thought of dragons sent a ripple of fear through her that was enough to make Turvina's eyes narrow. Desperate for a distraction, Sabine turned her attention to the Elder's long white hair. It had been arranged in an artful display of forty-two braids, accentuating the gentle slope of her pointed ears. Each braid had been plaited with flowers, crystal beads, and tiny silver bells that chimed whenever the woman moved. Sabine had spent the first few minutes repeatedly counting the plaits as they swung back and forth. Then she moved on to the flowers. The next hour had gone to the beads. Perhaps it was time to start on the bells.

"I heard Queen Mali'theoria is returning tomorrow to assess this latest undertaking. She was quite specific in her instructions about how your new power was to be harnessed." The ancient fae dipped her needle into the blood-infused ink on the nearby table. The metallic scent of blood and tangy ozone thickened the air, charging it with elemental power. The needle began to glow silver as Turvina instilled the magic needed to complete her work.

Sabine squeezed her eyes shut and braced for the next assault. Clenching her fists until her nails bit into her palms, she sent another silent request to the absent gods for endurance and strength. Sweat dripped down her face from the stifling heat and hours of pain she'd already endured.

"You've been marking Sabin'theoria's skin for nearly five hours now, Turvina," Giannia said from the far side of the room. "If your intention was to break the princess's will, you have failed. The Unseelie queen is not known for her forgiveness, and you risk much by extending her daughter's session beyond the sands in the glass."

Sabine blinked open her eyes, surprised by the sharpness of her tutor's words. Giannia stood near the crystal wall, her smoky lilac hair coiled into a modest knot at the nape of her neck. Her violet eyes glowed with restrained anger, and her nails had already sharpened into wicked talons.

Uh oh. Her night harpy side was showing. That never boded well.

Few dared risk offending Turvina, a fact the Elder seemed to relish. But Giannia had a point—and a fierce protective instinct.

If Sabine failed to complete this marking, Turvina's life might be forfeit. The Unseelie queen wouldn't tolerate any failure involving her heir, and she was ruthless in assigning blame. Sabine couldn't help but wonder if Turvina was intentionally courting death's embrace.

"Bah." Turvina waved off Giannia's warning. "If Sabin'theoria intends to be our queen one day, this is nothing compared to what she'll face. You don't see me complaining, and I've been the one etching her skin for hours. But if the princess isn't up to the sacrifice required to harness her abilities…"

The Elder's voice trailed off, but the threat and challenge in her eyes were clear. Sabine swallowed her reservations, determined to see it through.

"Finish it," she managed, biting out the words through clenched teeth. Giannia might mean well, but the last thing Sabine needed was gossip about her inability to control her magic. The fae didn't reward or respect weakness.

The Elder gave a faint nod of approval and drove the needle into Sabine's skin again. Agony rippled down her arm like molten glass, searing her soul as the blood-infused ink bound her power to the new markings. She squeezed her eyes shut, clamping down on the cry that threatened to betray her.

"That leaf design already captures the moon phases," Giannia murmured, her voice much closer now. "You've woven the lunar thread beautifully. If the princess can guide it with a mere drop of blood, what more is left to be done?"

Something hot and wet dripped from her arm, but she couldn't risk looking. Feeling it was one thing, but seeing it might push her over the edge. She had to focus on the purpose behind this trial.

All magic demanded a sacrifice, and this pain was hers. The ability to harness the moon's power was rare, coveted even among the Unseelie. Few outside the royal bloodlines ever possessed such a gift. She'd come into hers earlier than anyone expected, and it was critical she learn to master it. The alternative could plunge their world into darkness—not exactly the kind of footnote she wanted on a royal resume.

"Just a few finishing touches for our future queen," Turvina said, plucking a small white lendonian blossom from one of the braids in her hair. She pressed it to her lips, then blew across Sabine's arm, sending a sharp wave of power rippling through her. The ink pulsed, binding itself deeper into her skin. "I've infused the essence of night-blooming flowers into the mark. The gift of seduction runs strong in her line, but even those resistant to her charms will be swayed by the scent of our precious blooms."

"That's a Seelie ability," Giannia sputtered in shock. "Lendonian flowers or not, you're out of line, Turvina. Not only are you attempting to make our future queen beholden to you with this so-called *gift*, but you dare mark her with the sign of those gods-grovelers?"

Sabine's gaze drifted to the smoky ceiling. "Do not forget that I am part-Seelie by right of birth, Giannia. My loyalty lies with the Unseelie, but I carry both aspects of power. Even my mother uses lendonian oil in her arts. The flowers may be associated with the Seelie, but they prefer the light of the full moon."

"You are decades from reaching your majority, Princess," Giannia argued, her voice gruff and edged with concern. "The Council of Eight will not approve a consort until you claim your throne and reach your centennial. This sort of ornamentation was not sanctioned under Queen Mali'theoria's agreement with Elder Turvina."

Turvina gave a dismissive snort. "A debt may be settled at any time. And this gift will flourish as her power deepens."

"Our future queen is not some Seelie whore you can shackle with obligation."

Sabine flinched at Giannia's words, but Turvina waved a hand in silent reprimand to keep still. Sabine blew out a breath and shot her tutor a warning look, but she was focused on the Elder. With hands on her hips and a glare that could cut stone, Giannia looked ready to confiscate Turvina's needles.

Part of Sabine really hoped she would.

"Do you seek to deprive the girl of a future weapon in her arsenal?" Turvina asked, dipping her needles into the ink once more. "If those damned fools on the council follow the same path they did with our queen, they'll match Sabin'theoria with a Seelie husband. She'll need tremendous power to keep him under her heel."

"Don't blaspheme while the Seelie prince is still under our roof," Giannia snapped, her foot tapping against the magic-infused crystal floor. "If Prince Rhys or his guards were to overhear such a comment, we'll both be stripped of our titles and exiled by morning."

"Giannia, enough," Sabine said sharply. Discussions about her twin brother, Rhys, were a sore subject. It was taking everything she had to stay above the pain. "The hour grows late. Let Elder Turvina finish."

"As the princess wills it," Giannia muttered, stepping back with a stiff nod, though her jaw remained tight. Sabine squeezed her eyes shut again. She'd need to smooth things over with Giannia later, but surviving Turvina's torture-by-needle was her first priority.

Turvina harrumphed. "Your mother likely has a great many plans for future markings, but this gift will set you apart from most other rulers. Why, in a mere decade, you'll be able to turn the heads of even your greatest foes. You shall be adored, beloved… right up until the moment you crush them."

A hard lump formed in Sabine's throat. The idea of ruling was daunting. Fortunately, she had centuries before her mother would surrender her crown. Until then, she needed to learn and harness as much power as possible. The weak didn't survive long in Faerie, especially not under her mother's rule.

But first, she had to endure this marking and demonstrate the strength of will to wield such power. It was only the beginning of many trials yet to come.

Failure wouldn't just cost her the crown. She might be her mother's heir, but Sabine harbored no illusions. Queen Mali'theoria would murder her own daughter without hesitation if Sabine proved unworthy. She couldn't afford to ever forget that.

CHAPTER TWO

*A*nother hour crawled by before Turvina finally set down her needles.

"My work is complete, Your Highness," she announced, wiping her hands with a nearby cloth. "I'll be taking my leave now."

Sabine tried to sit up, but collapsed back against the lounge, her strength failing her. Black spots danced at the edges of her vision. Turvina had only marked her arm, but every part of her body throbbed.

She couldn't afford to faint. Not here. Not now. She had to reach her chambers before anyone noticed how close she was to breaking. Spies were everywhere.

Gritting her teeth, she braced her palms against the chair and tried again to push herself upright.

Giannia rushed to her side and slipped an arm around her shoulders, guiding her into a seated position. "Easy, Princess. Take it slow."

Sabine swallowed hard and leaned into her. Giannia steadied her, then reached for a pillow and wedged it behind her for support.

Once she was settled, Sabine motioned weakly toward the side table. "The box, if you will, Giannia."

Giannia hesitated only a moment before retrieving the small, jewel-encrusted crystal container and placing it in Sabine's lap.

It took several tries before Sabine managed to open the lid. A slender vial rested atop a bed of midnight-blue satin, its silver liquid shimmering like starlight.

Not trusting herself to lift the vial, she tilted the box toward Turvina, who was staring at it with undisguised longing.

"One of the last remaining vials of traverein," Sabine said. "It was blended with a single drop from the Well, gathered by Theoria herself before the Hall of the Gods was sealed. May it ease your hands… and settle the debt incurred by your *gift*."

Turvina pressed a hand to her mouth, eyes welling with tears. She dropped to her knees and bowed her head. "Your Highness, I am truly humbled by this offering. You have honored me more than I ever dreamed. I am forevermore in your debt."

"Rise, Elder Turvina," Sabine said, replacing the lid on the jeweled case and gesturing to her tutor.

Giannia stepped forward, retrieved the box, and quietly transferred it to Turvina's belongings. The older fae was shaking so badly, she might drop the vial before she could use it to heal her aching hands. Neither Sabine nor Giannia would shame her by acknowledging the raw, unguarded emotion. The traverein was one of the few relics left in the world able to heal any wound without stripping away the magic earned through sacrifice. It was priceless beyond measure.

Giannia collected Turvina's bag and led her to the door. As her tutor pressed the crystal panel embedded in the wall, the sealed doorway shimmered, then dissolved. A rush of fresh air spilled in from the garden beyond.

Sabine inhaled greedily, relieved to breathe something other than blood, magic, and incense. The room had been sealed to prevent foreign enchantments from interfering with the skin etching.

Giannia passed Turvina's bag to a waiting servant. As the Elder stepped into the corridor, one of Sabine's guards moved forward. He cast a quick glance in Sabine's direction, then leaned toward Giannia to speak in a low voice.

Judging by the fervent whispers and the guard's rigid posture, something had happened while she'd been locked inside the meditation chamber.

Sabine flung her silk robe over her shoulders, wincing as the enchanted fabric clung momentarily to her raw skin. The threads were woven to mold to the wearer's aura, and hers was a tangle of magic and pain.

Until her power returned and she could weave glamour that didn't ripple like pond water in a windstorm, she'd have to rely on mundane means to hide the design. If the wrong eyes caught a glimpse, whispers would spread before she reached her chambers. Secrecy was paramount. Visibility meant vulnerability.

Giannia turned, her expression grim. "Your beastman protector has been unavoidably delayed."

Sabine stiffened and looked to the guard for confirmation. He gave a terse nod. Balkin wasn't merely a guard. He was her blood-bonded shield, a trusted advisor, and one of the few she considered family. He should have been here—especially now, when she was at her weakest and her mother was absent from court.

Tension between the Seelie and Unseelie had been escalating for months. Sabine's naming as heir had only sharpened the divide, especially with her twin brother soon to denounce his ties to her court. Every step she took, every breath she drew, felt balanced on the edge of war.

"What's happened, Vaelor?"

The guard bowed low. "Forgive the intrusion, Your Highness. The Seelie guards have crossed the borders into our lands under the guise of protecting their future heir. They came nearly two hundred strong. Commander Balkin is attempting to keep order in Queen Mali'theoria's absence. He has entrusted your safety to your personal guards."

Sabine frowned, understanding the implications immediately. "My brother hasn't renounced his ties to the Unseelie yet. Even when he does, the treaties only allow a score of Seelie guards within the palace. They wouldn't have dared such a move if my mother was here. Where are the excess guards camped?"

Vaelor's eyes gleamed with approval at her insight. "The interlopers are stationed along the eastern forest's edge. At present, you have only five guards as your personal escort. The others have been called away to keep the Seelie at bay. Commander Balkin bids you return to your quarters until he or Queen Mali'theoria can relieve us."

Sabine's mouth thinned. If the moon phase hadn't demanded this etching be done today, they would have waited until more allies were in the palace. She was far too exposed. They all were. Of all the nights for the Seelie to push their boundaries, it had to be the one where her power was as steady as a goblin walking a tightrope.

"I'll be ready in a moment, Vaelor," Sabine said, tying the sash around her waist.

"Our captain is securing the wards. Once he gives the all-clear, we'll be ready to depart."

Sabine inclined her head. After he'd retreated, she turned to Giannia. "Is it possible my mother's return is what stirred the commotion at the borders?"

"We can only hope. If that's the case, the strength of her escort will give the Seelie pause. We can't afford to take chances. We must heed Vaelor's warning and get you to safety. The wards around your wing are among the strongest in the palace. Your guards can defend from there."

Sabine nodded.

Giannia slipped an arm around Sabine and helped her stand. "We should take the back stairways, Princess. There are fewer watchful eyes."

Sabine's vision swam, her knees threatening to buckle. Giannia tightened her grip, keeping her upright. Fortunately, her tutor was stronger than she appeared.

"I won't fool anyone for long," Sabine murmured. "My magic's too depleted for complicated glamour. Tarron may need to act as my escort. He's done it often enough that few will question it."

"You must walk on your own power," Giannia whispered urgently. "Other than your personal escort, the guards and servants on this level aren't blood-sworn. They'll spread gossip faster than the wind carries pollen to the pixies. You cannot appear weakened in front of them."

Sabine gave a barely discernible nod. With Giannia close enough to steady her if she faltered, she began her slow march toward the door. With each step, she inhaled and exhaled, using her breath to time her movements.

As she crossed the threshold, her guard captain approached. With hair the color of fallen leaves and pale green eyes, Tarron'ethos looked more like one of the forest fae than the noble lineage his name proclaimed. It didn't hurt that he preferred the raw practicality of underworld-forged gear over the polished gleam of courtly armor. There was something in that dangerous edge that always caused Sabine's heart to skip a beat.

"Princess," Tarron said and swept his gaze over her, lingering a fraction longer than decorum suggested. He touched his knuckle first to his forehead, and then to his chest. The first gesture acknowledged her power. The second was an oath from the heart. "I trust you're well?"

Sabine smiled and placed her hand on his arm, infusing her touch with a trace of magic. "It's good to see you, Tarron."

"The moon always shines more radiantly in your presence, my princess," he murmured, bowing his head briefly in response to her magical offering. Sabine squeezed his arm before releasing him. At his signal, the others closed around her in a protective formation.

"You shouldn't encourage him," Giannia said after weaving a quick barrier to prevent anyone from over-hearing their conversation. "He already has ambitions of becoming your consort. Rumor has it his family is courting councilors to raise the matter with the queen."

Sabine's smile faded. She hadn't given much thought to consorts—or ruling, beyond surviving court politics. The idea of someone maneuvering for her hand felt distant, theoretical. Still... her eyes followed Tarron's retreating form, admiring the quiet confidence in his stride, and the way his hand never strayed far from the hilt at his hip. Her gaze lingered a moment too long before she caught herself. She darted a quick glance at Giannia, who was regarding her with a chastising look. Sabine inwardly sighed. Perhaps she *had* shown him more favor than she realized.

He'd been among the first to swear loyalty to her after

she was named heir. In Balkin's absence, Tarron had become her shield and sword—and friend. But such ties were often weaknesses, or so her mother had warned her time and again.

Several servants and palace guards lined the corridor, all eyes drifting toward her as she passed. The faint glamour she used to conceal her exhaustion was already sparking a dull headache. Walking was like wading upstream through mud, each step a conscious effort to stay upright.

Bioluminescent vines clung to the arched ceiling over-head, their blossoms pulsing softly with light. Faerie lanterns shaped like glassy seedpods and strung with veins of living crystal cast dancing shadows along the moon-stone floor.

"We should have been finished hours ago, but that foolish woman was determined to gain the advantage," Giannia muttered, leading Sabine slowly down the hall.

Their padded slippers were silent against the polished flooring, though faint musical tones chimed with each step. The enchantment woven into the corridor's founda-tion responded to her presence like a sentinel announcing the arrival of the Unseelie heir. It sounded pretty, but it made sneaking around the palace a nightmare.

Sabine nodded at a few nobles as she walked, keeping her expression carefully neutral. Her skin prickled with awareness beneath the weight of so many stares. Everyone they passed watched her closely, hoping to glimpse the new markings that would provide a hint of her emerging abilities.

Giannia fixed a pleasant smile on her face and murmured, "Turvina never expected your 'offering' to turn her so neatly back into your family's debt. Her grandchil-dren will be repaying that favor for generations."

"That was my mother's intention," Sabine muttered, staggering slightly as dark spots crept into her vision again. Her stomach lurched with a fresh wave of nausea.

Giannia wrapped a stabilizing wave of magic around her, preventing her from falling. Sabine took a deep breath and pushed it aside with a wave of her hand. She *would* walk on her own power—both physical and metaphysical.

"How did you know to bring the vial of traverein? Her agreement to harness your magic had already been negotiated and bartered."

Sabine gave a polite nod to a troll she'd met at dinner the night before. His name was Karwin—No. Kavin. Kathin? Ugh. She was too tired for this.

"I thought Elder Turvina might attempt something in my mother's absence. Turns out, I was right."

"We're nearly there," Giannia warned softly, her smile never faltering. "Just through the courtyard now."

Tarron raised his hand to signal the other guards to sweep the area, but Sabine caught his arm before he could step forward. A familiar ripple of magic brushed against her senses.

Her breath hitched as a pair of voices drifted upon the garden breeze. It was Rhys… and someone else.

"Power favors those who reach for it, not those who wait meekly at the border, Your Highness."

"Do not mistake a predator's stalking for complacency, Councilor. When I strike, I fully intend to step into the light."

A pause. "And if another stands where you were meant to rise, Your Highness?"

"Then I'll rise higher—and grind the challengers to dust."

Sabine narrowed her eyes and straightened. Her brother's words echoed like a dagger drawn in shadow. She didn't know who he was speaking with, but the conversation strayed dangerously close to treason.

In Faerie, meaning often mattered less than how others chose to hear it. The fae couldn't lie, but that simply meant they knew how to dance on the edge of that blade.

So be it. She intended to dance.

CHAPTER THREE

arron and the other guards snapped to attention, their magic rising as they fell into formation around her. If she didn't end this quickly, blood would be spilled. Sabine barely breathed as she rounded the corner, her steps soundless on the stone.

"I applaud your resolve, Prince Rhys," the man said, his voice casual—too casual. "The Seelie remember who bled for the gods and who chose to flee into darkness. The blood of loyalty still holds weight."

"Does it?" Sabine asked mildly. "And here I thought the Unseelie's strength was in their refusal to remain play-things for the Tuatha Dé."

Rhys turned first, straightening. The drifting lanterns cast a soft gleam over his silvery-white hair, but they also highlighted the dark circles beneath his eyes that not even his glamour could hide. His expression flickered with surprise, guilt, and a flash of something unreadable. He opened his mouth, but said nothing.

Sabine resisted the urge to ease the shadows plaguing her brother. He wouldn't welcome such interference—or her acknowledging any signs of weakness. Instead, she turned a cold glare on the man beside him. He was a powerful figure, his calculating gaze assessing her as if he'd known she was there all along.

One of the Council of Eight.

The Councilor tilted his head to regard her, his braided, seashell-blue hair falling nearly to his waist. The Waykeeper, if Sabine remembered correctly. He was one of the few council members who regularly straddled both courts yet made little effort to hide his Seelie allegiance. Her mother had complained about him often enough that Sabine half expected him to be covered in warts and swamp slime.

Instead, his skin gleamed like carved pink opal and his oversized silver-violet eyes eerily reminded her of a cat. He wore layered robes stitched with silvery thread in the shape of runes that shifted and rearranged themselves when the breeze rustled the cloth. Appropriate, given his position, she supposed. But the peculiar movement was doing little to help with her headache.

The Waykeeper's gaze swept over her, his eyes lingering on her covered arm a little too long. "You've returned from the marking, I see. Still whole? Or only mostly?"

His words were honeyed, but the sting beneath them was barbed.

Tarron narrowed his eyes and stepped forward, his hand resting on the hilt of his sword. His skin began to glow as power enveloped him in warning. "You stand on Unseelie land and address Princess Sabin'theoria, Heir to the Unseelie Throne. You are not granted leave to speak to her thus—not here, and not without consequence."

The Councilor's lip curled. "Princess."

Schooling her features into the neutral court mien she often wore like armor, Sabine inclined her head. "I am whole enough to recognize a blade dressed in silk, Councilor—as do my guards." Her gaze drifted to the thorned vines slithering through the garden gravel. "A word of advice: our roses don't take kindly to trespassers, or those who disparage the Unseelie. They tend to bite. Step lightly."

A faint smile tugged at the Waykeeper's lips, but his eyes flashed with some unnamed emotion. Whether it was amusement or condescension, she couldn't tell. Nor was she inclined to care. It was taking every last bit of her strength to pretend she hadn't just endured several hours of grueling torture.

Rhys took a step toward her, his expression concerned. "I thought you would have already been finished by now."

Sabine's smile softened. "No. Were you waiting for me?"

Rhys's hands curled briefly before relaxing. "I came out to get some air."

Sabine tilted her head. Not a lie. Not quite the truth. Fae learned early how to walk that line.

Sabine glanced at the Councilor, wondering why he was there—especially when her mother was absent. That worried her, more than the creeping flowers that looked like they were about to make a meal of the Waykeeper's blood. She flicked her wrist toward them, halting their progress. The vines trembled but remained still.

Good boys.

She focused again on the Councilor. "I trust your discussion is concluded?"

"It was enlightening," the Waykeeper said smoothly. "The future always is." He inclined his head. "Prince Rhys'ellesar. Princess Sabin'theoria. With your permission, I'll take my leave."

Sabine gave him a curt nod. As the Councilor strode

away, Rhys's shoulders sagged and he pinched the bridge of his nose. He sighed and lifted his head, his raw and unguarded expression cutting her to the quick.

"Are you here to gloat?"

Sabine's brow furrowed, her composure slipping. "What?"

Rhys straightened and gestured to her arm. "Your mark. That's how many now?"

Sabine frowned and shook her head. "We were heading toward the back staircase. I—"

Giannia cleared her throat. "Forgive me, Your Highnesses. Perhaps you would consider finishing your conversation in your quarters?"

Rhys's gaze flew to Giannia and then to the small crowd gathering beyond the garden. He muttered a curse, the tips of his pointed ears reddening.

Holding out his arm, he said, "Allow me to escort you, sister."

She slipped her arm into his, grateful she didn't fall on her face. In a low voice, she murmured, "You shouldn't have been speaking with him. Not alone. Where are your guards?"

Rhys's jaw tightened. "They're not your concern. I can handle myself."

Sabine hesitated, then softened her tone. "I think he was testing you—us. And I think he enjoyed it. Rhys, you have to be careful. If you give anyone a reason to suspect—"

He gave a short, bitter laugh. "You don't think I know that? A few more hours. Then I'm done playing the Unseelie puppet."

She studied him from the corner of her eye. "Is that what you think you are?"

Rhys didn't answer. His steps slowed as they neared the

courtyard gates. In a voice barely audible, he murmured, "I don't know what I am anymore."

A tingle of magic coated the air.

Sabine's steps faltered. She glanced at Rhys, only to find him pausing as well, his nostrils flaring. The cloying scent of sweetened pollen drifted on the air, a shimmer of gold that floated across the garden path.

Tarron shouted something from behind them, and one of the guards slammed his hand on the ground. Dark shadows erupted from the earth, forming a protective barrier around them.

"Don't breathe," Rhys warned, grabbing her arm.

But it was too late.

Rhys staggered beside her, his hand clutching his throat. Sabine choked as the sweetness turned acrid, already burning her lungs. Something sharp unfurled beneath her skin, threading up her neck like thorned ivy. Her fingers clawed at her throat and came away wet with blood. She could feel the Seelie magic blooming within her, venomous and twining through her blood like it had been waiting for her. It would suffocate them in minutes.

Rhys dropped to one knee, coughing violently. Black vines mottled the skin beneath his jaw, blooming in spirals like ink spilled through water. She dropped beside him, her knees scraping against the garden stones. Rhys reached out to her, his eyes wide with panic and fear.

She couldn't scream. There was no breath.

"*Velari!*" Giannia shouted and clapped her hands together, a lavender dome forming overhead. The gold pollen floated sluggishly now, pressing against the barrier like it had a mind of its own.

It was too late. She could already feel it leeching the magic from her.

No.

She refused to die here.

Sabine pressed her bloody hand against the ground and reached for the land's essence. Power that came from an ancient, dormant part of her soul surged on instinct, burning through her markings. She wordlessly called to the roses and demanded they *hunt*. Not even glamour would hide the infiltrator from their thorns. This was *her* land and place of power.

The vines struck.

From the far side of the courtyard, a scream rang out.

One of the guards shouted, "There!"

Tarron stepped forward, his skin glowing like moonlight against the darkness of his armor. He lifted a hand and snapped his fingers. The sound cracked like a bone breaking.

A cloaked figure stumbled from the shadows, gasping. His limbs twisted, bones snapping backward, joints crumpling like paper as Tarron unleashed his magic. Another of her guards lifted his hands, daggers of darkness shooting from his palms and striking the assassin. He collapsed to the ground with a wet, muffled shriek as his bones liquefied and seeped into the ground.

Sabine didn't flinch.

She had no breath left.

Giannia dropped to the ground beside her, her hands glowing as she pressed her fingers to Sabine's chest and Rhys's arm.

"*Tenaren!*" she hissed, slowing the progress of the magic. Sabine's vision blurred at the edges. Her throat burned, but her heartbeat slowed, no longer spiked by panic. The twisting bloom of poison hesitated, faltered.

"I need the tonic from my bag! Now!" Giannia snapped.

One of the guards sprinted to retrieve her satchel from where it had fallen near the courtyard steps.

"Sabin—" Rhys croaked. His skin was pale, his lips tinged gray. She gripped his arm, mentally willing him to keep fighting.

Giannia shoved a vial between her lips, the liquid sharp and bitter as it coated her tongue. Sabine gagged, but swallowed it down.

The black ivy on her neck recoiled, and she took a full breath. She grabbed the bottle and tipped the remaining liquid into Rhys's mouth.

"Princess, it's Unseelie—" Giannia began.

"Drink," she urged Rhys, her throat still raw from the dwindling magic. She gripped his arm tightly, infusing the vestiges of her strength into her touch. Unseelie tonic or not, she would not allow her brother to die. Her power would soften the effects, reinforcing his ties to the light. Another wave of dizziness washed over her, but she battled it back. She couldn't pass out. Not yet.

He gulped the liquid greedily, his eyes watering from the magic. The black ivy on his skin began to fade, and he coughed. His fingers tightened briefly around her wrist. "I thought—when the magic hit—you…"

Sabine let out a relieved breath and shook her head. She squeezed his hand briefly before releasing him. They needed answers.

Tarron approached the assassin crumpled on the ground and pressed a knee to his chest. As he yanked him upward, Sabine caught sight of a symbol etched upon the fae's skin, just below his throat. It pulsed silver, almost vibrating with a building intensity.

Sabine's breath caught. "Tarron!"

The body jerked, and his mark detonated. A searing burst of light erupted from the assassin's neck, so bright it painted the courtyard white.

When the light faded, Tarron stood over a scorched imprint on the ground. No body. No bones. No answers.

Only ash.

Tarron turned to meet her eyes, his expression hard, but the set of his jaw betrayed more than anger. Power still hummed beneath his skin as he stalked toward her, the weight of unspent vengeance sharp in the air while the other guards fanned out to search the courtyard.

They wouldn't find anything. She knew it as well as they did. But there was no doubt who sent this assassin—her father.

A flash of guilt enveloped Sabine. Tarron and the others would have secured the garden before she entered, if she hadn't been so intent on interrupting the Councilor's conversation with Rhys.

She forced her gaze away from Tarron and turned back to her brother. Rhys sat up and rubbed his neck, staring at the darkened patch on the ground where the assassin had died. "One more day, and then I'm done with this farce..."

Sabine shook her head and reached for Rhys. "What makes you think this will stop once you denounce your ties to the Unseelie, Rhys? You were as much a target as me. My blood runs through your veins, as yours does in mine. That magic was targeted specifically to our bloodline, not Giannia's, nor Tarron's, nor—"

Rhys pulled away and pushed off the ground. "Yes, but once I'm no longer tied to the Unseelie, my loyalties will no longer be split, and the servants won't hesitate to offer me a tonic. Will they, *sister*?"

Sabine didn't respond. There wasn't anything she could say. He was right, and that realization only served to widen the divide between them. Even if she ordered every guard and servant in the palace to protect him, they would obey, but only up to a point.

Rhys was expendable.

His shoulders drooped. "Sabina, I didn't..." His voice cut off. In a voice that was as quiet as a whisper, he murmured, "I'm glad you're all right."

Tarron stepped between them and offered Sabine his hand. She took it, allowing him to pull her to her feet. Another wave of dizziness swept over her, but she tried to blink it back and focus on her brother. Tarron wrapped his arm around her waist to keep her steady, a thin coat of glamour brushing against her as he hid his assistance from sight.

"Princess?"

She shook her head, continuing to focus on her brother. "Where are your guards, Rhys? They should have been here protecting you."

Rhys's jaw clenched. "Apparently, they've been called away to investigate a 'situation' on the border."

Sabine stared at him. "On whose order?"

In a low voice, Tarron murmured, "I'll see to the investigation myself, Your Highness. Your brother will not be left unguarded. But first, we must get you safely away to your chambers."

Giannia nodded. "We are gathering too much attention."

Sabine took a deep breath and nodded. "Have Vaelor act as Rhys's escort until this matter is resolved."

"At once, Your Highness," Tarron said, nodding toward Vaelor.

Rhys opened his mouth and then closed it. He tilted his head in acknowledgment of her order before turning away and heading toward the growing group of curious onlookers hovering at the edge of the courtyard. They greeted him with smiling faces, likely eager to hear any scraps of gossip he was willing to divulge. Vaelor would keep him safe. And distance from her would hopefully keep him safer yet.

He lifted his head to meet her eyes for a moment. In that instant, she saw the sadness and loneliness that surrounded him like a shroud. A second later, it was gone, replaced again by the court mask that hid his true emotions from the world.

She stared after him, wishing there were some way of bridging the rift between them. They both knew she was the true target of the assassin's attack, and he was simply collateral damage. But knowing that didn't make it easier to swallow. Until he denounced the Unseelie side of his heritage, both courts would continue to view him as either a possible threat… or a pawn.

CHAPTER FOUR

"Princess," Tarron said, his voice gentle. "We must get you to your chambers."

She nodded and leaned against him, allowing him to support her weight. Tarron's body was solid beneath her touch, steady in a way she hadn't realized she needed after dealing with the assassin.

The junction to the back stairwell shimmered ahead, half-concealed behind a lattice of silver mist and hanging twilight blossoms that only parted for those with the proper bloodline. She just needed to make it a bit farther, then she could rest.

Gods, why hadn't she remembered to coax one of the living lifts closer to this wing before her marking? The older wings of the palace resisted change, and the lift-vines only responded to bloodline and will. Even if she opened a vein, there was no way she could concentrate enough to summon one now.

"The Waykeeper is up to something, and I suspect your brother is at the heart of it," Giannia murmured. "I wouldn't be surprised if he invited the assassin into the palace, using the preparation for Rhys's ceremony tomorrow as a way to smuggle him inside."

"You might be right," Sabine said, her voice quieting as they approached the stairway. A small brownie wearing a simple tunic of forest green was scrubbing the floor with a thistle brush. She hummed a wordless melody, leaving faint trails of sparkles that vanished with each stroke.

Giannia beckoned to the brownie. The diminutive fae scrambled upright and darted toward them, her bare feet silent against the crystalline floor. The guards scowled at her but allowed her to pass. She lifted her head with an eager smile, darting a quick glance at Sabine before averting her gaze.

Her dark, weathered skin had the appearance of worn leather, but her brown eyes danced with vigor and intelligence. Brownies often kept to the shadows for survival's sake, but they couldn't suppress their longing to be close to sidhe magic. It was one of the hallmarks of all lesser fae.

Though she stood scarcely thigh-high, the brownie bowed low and asked, "How may I serve you?"

Giannia flicked her fingers, releasing a pale blue stream of magic that coiled gently around the brownie like a ribbon. "Send refreshments to the princess's quarters, and alert her attendants she's returned and wishes to rest. She is not to be disturbed."

"At once, my lady," the woman said and leaped to her feet. The bucket of soapy water disappeared in a puff of bubbles and light. The brownie turned and sprinted down the hall, her dark wispy hair flying behind her.

"With your permission, Princess?" Tarron asked, his voice low and warm against her ear.

She swallowed and nodded.

His magic swirled around her, cloaking her as he lifted her into his arms. She leaned her head against his shoulder as he carried her up the stairs. At least she didn't have to worry about falling while he held her.

At the top of the stairs, he lowered her to the ground but didn't release her immediately. Instead, he swept his gaze over her, his hand lingering on her waist. His magic brushed over her skin in a questioning whisper, though the quiet intensity in his eyes hinted at words left unsaid.

"I'm all right, Tarron," she said with a soft smile. "Just tired."

"I can handle things from here, Captain," Giannia said crisply.

"Of course." Tarron bowed and squeezed her hand gently. "Rest well, Princess."

He turned back to the stairwell, vanishing behind the shimmer of the wards. She missed his strength almost immediately but refused to call him back. It was unlikely he'd discover much about the assassin, but they had to try. At the very least, her guards would ensure Rhys wouldn't encounter the Councilor alone again.

Leaning on Giannia, Sabine made her way down the long hallway reserved for the royal family. Here, there was no need for subterfuge. The queen's suites occupied the level above, but this one belonged to her and Rhys, and their blood-sworn servants. Every doorway was sealed to all but the royal family, their personal guards, and those bound to them by blood oath.

Giannia kept her pace slow, her arm wrapped around Sabine's waist. "You *should* rest. That display took more from you than you're willing to admit."

Sabine gave a bitter laugh, too weary to mask the edge in her voice. "Which display? The ritual torture, the political theater, or the assassin?"

Giannia didn't answer. Her violet eyes flicked back to the stairwell, but the hallway was empty or any would-be listeners. "We expected the Seelie to strike while you're at your weakest, but the Councilor wasn't expected—especially seconds before the attack. You've dealt with Elders before. But that one... he's dangerous. And far too bold. Tread lightly, Princess."

Sabine's steps faltered. "He's one of the Council of Eight. They're all dangerous."

"Yes, but for more reasons than you might realize. No one joins the Eight without blood on their hands. If the Waykeeper arrived while Queen Mali'theoria is absent, plots are already in motion. I fear what this might mean for you."

Sabine's brow furrowed. Something about the Waykeeper's assessing gaze had unsettled her, as if he already knew her secrets. Her position as Heir protected her in some ways, but it also painted a target on her back. And Rhys...

He was a Seelie prince adrift among those who scorned the light he wielded.

Giannia's voice lowered. "There are whispers that the Council may be... repositioning pieces. Waiting to see where your brother lands. Some even claim the duality of your magic is a sign his Seelie gifts were usurped. It would explain his lack of power compared to your own."

Sabine's mouth tightened. "You dare repeat such falsehoods?"

Giannia stopped, her grip on Sabine tightening. Her violet eyes blazed. "Never. But I fear what Prince Rhys may believe—especially if those whispers come from King Cadan'ellesar's inner circle."

A sick feeling rose inside her. "Then I need to speak with my brother. Tonight."

Giannia hesitated. "You're in no condition—"

"This can't wait. If the Waykeeper is bold enough to

speak openly while on Unseelie soil, we may already be too late. And if he brought the assassin with him…" She shook her head. "I need to know if my brother was also a target or simply in the wrong place at the wrong time. I'm protected, but Rhys is not."

Now more than ever, Sabine wished Balkin were here. She was beyond exhausted, her thoughts fuzzy and unclear. But she needed to talk to her brother before things deteriorated even more. Gods. If these rumors were circulating and they believed Rhys to be weak, her father might want to arrange an accident before he could ever tarnish the Seelie's light.

"Princess, it may be hours until he returns to his quarters. You're not strong enough to wait—"

"I know my limitations," Sabine said, pressing her hand to the wall. "I'll leave him a note and ask him to meet me for dinner. That should give me a few hours to rest."

Hopefully by then, she'd have an idea of how to get him to open up to her. And how to keep him alive.

They stopped at the entrance to Rhys's rooms, the carved wardstones glowing faintly.

"I'll wait here until you're finished," Giannia said softly.

Sabine gave her a nod, brushing her fingers over the sigil etched into the doorway. It flared softly in response to her touch, and the wards parted.

Thick rugs overtop the crystal floor muffled her steps as she entered. The suite was a world apart from the rest of the palace. Sunlight poured through tall arched windows, casting golden light across walls of soft cream and blue. Vines climbed a spiral column toward the second-level loft, where an indoor garden was nestled with colorful blooms.

It was Seelie through and through.

Their mother hated it.

She crossed to his desk, cluttered with books on magical theory, principles of divination, and even gardening. An open tome caught her attention, its margins crowded with Rhys's familiar script. She drew it closer, recognizing the topic at once.

"Manifestation delays in magic and the influence of emotional stasis on power thresholds," Sabine read aloud.

"Oh, Rhys," she murmured, sinking into the chair. "Your magic isn't dormant. I feel it within you."

His gifts had always been quieter than hers. His magic was subtle and controlled, where hers always felt wild, like stormwinds battling from within. She often wondered if something in her was broken. Why did her power surge with so little provocation, while Rhys's unfolded like sunlight through stained glass?

She reached for a sheet of parchment, but movement caught her eye. A faint shimmer of light reflected off the polished floor. Tilting her head, she crouched and pushed aside the chair.

A sliver of crystal, no longer than her thumbnail, was wedged into the wood near the underside of the drawer. It swirled with green and purple magic.

Sabine's breath caught.

A listening shard.

They were banned in private quarters, especially in royal wings. Only those with ill intent planted them where family spoke in confidence.

Sabine worried her lower lip. Was her mother so concerned about Rhys's growing ties to the Seelie court that she'd begun spying on him? No one other than blood-sworn servants were able to enter this part of the palace. Not even Giannia dared enter without Rhys's direct permission.

Her stomach twisted. Perhaps this was what Rhys

meant about not being an Unseelie puppet. Had he discovered the shard? If he hadn't redecorated his suite to be more in line with his Seelie tastes, Sabine never would have noticed the reflection.

She squeezed her eyes shut, her loyalty to her court and brother warring within her. She might be destined to rule the Unseelie, but Rhys was more than her brother. He was her twin. In a place where he had few allies, she had to protect him. He would do the same for her. She had to believe that.

She opened her eyes and reached for the quill.

Dinner. She would ask him to share a meal, feel him out, and then… What? Ask him if he knew how a listening shard had found its way into his room? Ask him why the Councilor had cornered him?

Ask him if he truly believed the lies suggesting she'd stolen his magic?

The whole thing was maddening. Sabine brushed the feathered end of the phoenix feather against her chin, trying to rein in her temper. Rhys hadn't seemed overly concerned about his absent guards if he was roaming the palace freely. Perhaps there *was* a reason for their mother to monitor him.

"Princess?" Giannia called from the doorway. "Are you well?"

"A moment," Sabine called, reaching for the ink. She quickly penned the note inviting him to dinner, adjusted the book to where it had been, and stood.

She'd done what she could.

The first step was getting him to the table.

CHAPTER FIVE

Sabine didn't make it to dinner.

She barely made it to her rooms.

By the time she collapsed onto the velvet cushions, her body had already begun to shut down. Her limbs refused to move, her thoughts dulled, and magic slipped from her grasp like water through cracked glass.

She wasn't sure how much time had passed before she surfaced again. It was always disorienting when awakening after a healing slumber. She'd heard stories about the same thing happening to Theoria, her namesake and First of the Fae. It didn't make it any easier.

Sabine sat up and rubbed her eyes, the silk of her robe clinging to her skin. She winced and peeled it off, flexing her sore arm. Giannia must have removed her shoes, dimmed the lights, and drawn the curtains. Knowing her tutor, she had likely stayed for a while before retiring to her quarters at the end of the hall.

Magic pooled into her hands, and she absently threaded power through the Faerie lanterns that danced overhead. They brightened, casting a warm glow over her chambers.

It worried her sometimes, how easily the darkness stole her away. But her mother had always been dismissive about her concerns.

"The strongest powers burn the brightest," Sabine quoted her mother with a sigh. *"Even the stars need rest."*

Still… it didn't *feel* like rest. It was like losing herself. At the very least, losing hours or even days. The idea of being helpless and powerless like that sent a shiver of fear through her. If she hadn't made it back to her room in time… There were too many potential enemies surrounding her and too few she trusted.

She shook her head. At least Giannia had been here to make sure she didn't end up on the floor. That had happened on more than one occasion.

When she'd tried talking to Averia about the healing sleep, her friend had just looked puzzled. Apparently, most "normal" fae didn't stumble around passing out when they used too much power. She was the lucky one to be descended from gods. Yay. Go her. Just one more peculiarity with her magic.

A cup of tea sat on her nightstand, a timed enchantment keeping it gently warm. She took a sip of the rich, earthy brew and set it aside. There was something important…

Rhys.

She swung her legs over the side of the couch and staggered to the nearest curtain. With a flick of her fingers, she parted the fabric and peered out into the night.

Moonlight silvered the edge of the forest.

Sabine muttered a curse and pressed her hand against the carved crystal panes. If Rhys had tried to meet her for dinner and she hadn't shown, such neglect might have damaged their relationship even more. She could try to talk to him, to explain. But judging by the moon's high position in the sky, Rhys had likely been abed for hours.

He kept Seelie hours.

She turned from the window, a faint shiver sliding through her. The warmth from the lanterns did little to chase away the cold that settled over her. She'd have to wait to broach the subject of the listening crystal and her suspicions about the Waykeeper.

Thoughts of the listening crystal made her pause. She quickly walked over to her desk and peered underneath. A green and purple glimmer caught her eye.

No. It couldn't be. The same magic, the same swirling hues... here too?

Sabine hesitated and then reached out, her fingers brushing against the warm crystal. It pulsed briefly before resuming its normal swirling pattern. The rush of betrayal threatened to steal her breath.

Who? The queen? But why?

She replayed every conversation of the past week in her head. There was nothing of consequence, except discussions about her marking and Rhys's upcoming renouncement. Still, the sanctity of her rooms had been violated. She curled her fingers into a fist, battling the urge to shatter the crystal on the spot.

No. She had to think this through. There were too many implications to risk hasty action. Perhaps there was a way to turn the crystal against whoever had planted it.

As she stood, a rolled note on her desk caught her eye. The shadow wren must have come while she was unconscious. Hoping it was from Rhys, she reached for the sealed parchment and broke the enchantment with a touch of her magic.

Averia's delicate script covered the page.

Dearest Sabin'theoria,

I stopped by earlier, but your captain of the guard was playing the role of stoic sentinel. Alas, denied at your door—though Tarron'ethos has certainly grown into his armor. I could almost forgive the dismissal, had he smiled once. Almost.

The palace has been in an uproar, naturally. Whispers fly like shadow wrens about a laughable assassination attempt (bold, but sloppy), and Elder Turvina's delayed departure. Rumor says she claimed you'll leave a mark on the world far deeper than the one she inked on your skin. I do hope you'll tell me what she meant by that.

Prince Rhys'ellesar was in attendance for at least some of it. I'm told he left before the moon climbed high. His demeanor left the courtiers guessing, but I suspect you won't have to. He's always been far too transparent around you. I daresay I might even miss your brother once he's gone. The little storm clouds that follow in his wake do make court life so much more interesting.

Please tell me everything went well with Elder Turvina. I would love some hint as to her latest creation. Everyone has been speculating about your new mark and the power you've been gifted.

I eagerly await your speedy response.

-A

Sabine's heart thudded, wondering if she could even

risk trusting Averia. Her gaze lowered to her left arm, where the thorned vine marking curled around her wrist and climbed gracefully toward her shoulder. Of all her markings, it was the most captivating—second only to the one etched along her hip.

Each leaf bore an elemental signature, woven with magic and sealed with her blood. One of the leaves had the phases of the moon hidden within each vein, which shifted to reflect the passage of time. Another one held the memories of the forest. With it, she could not only control the passage of the moon, but also elicit the ancient memories of her ancestors.

It was a remarkable work of art, but the one she treasured the most was Elder Turvina's 'gift'. When she pressed her nose to her arm, she caught the faint scent of night-blooming flowers. In a palace that focused on every aspect of being Unseelie, this small defiance took root in Sabine's soul.

She frowned, momentarily gripped by uncertainty.

Each new marking brought her closer to her destiny. Whatever that was. And even worse, she didn't feel equipped for any of it.

Fortunately, her mother wasn't here to witness her doubts. And Sabine would never speak them aloud and risk the words being carried to an unseen listener.

Despite the mark's beauty, Sabine could still feel the burning agony from the needles sliding under her skin. The pain would linger for weeks or even months, a constant reminder that all magic came at a price.

Once the swelling faded, she could begin to determine how best to wield these new gifts. Until then, she needed to stay out of sight. Her mother would likely want to show it off like the others at some ball or formal function.

And Rhys would be conspicuously absent after tomorrow.

Sabine squeezed her eyes shut. She dreaded those functions, almost as much as the knowledge that every smile directed her way came with a hidden blade. Once she moved permanently to the Unseelie Palace, things would be even worse. At least here in the Winter Palace, she didn't have to deal with the constant influx of unfamiliar fae courtiers, or the hundreds of other Unseelie determined to curry her mother's favor.

There, it would simply be more people who wanted her dead. And not even her brother would be at her side as a welcome ally.

With a sigh, Sabine sat down and quickly penned a neutral reply to Averia, offering to meet her in the gardens after Rhys's renouncement ceremony. She wouldn't be able to show her the mark, but a few hints here and there would suffice.

She picked up a vial of pixie dust and sprinkled it over the note to seal the ink. Averia was decades older, but she'd only received two marks compared to Sabine's fourteen. The two of them had spent hours poring over the archivists' tomes, studying illustrations of Elder Turvina's past creations. Turvina's etchings were among the most coveted in Faerie, both for their artistry and the power they infused.

She just wished they didn't hurt so much, or that each one didn't feel like it carved away a sliver of her soul. Any enthusiasm for her marking had long since fled. Reality was a harsh mistress.

"The price of beauty and power, I suppose," Sabine murmured and sealed the note with a trace of magic.

She rose from her chair and opened her window, allowing the cool night air to flow into her room. A small silver collection plate rested on the windowsill, enchanted to summon the court messengers. Sabine carefully placed the note on its surface and traced her finger around the plate's rim. Sending a brief flare of power outward, she watched as a shadow wren swooped down, its feather rippling like smoke as it collected the message.

It was a beautiful night, like most in Faerie. Summer was nearing its end, and the leaves would be turning soon. From her third-floor window, Sabine could see the green fires of Seelie magic burning along the border as they waited to escort their prince back to their lands. The flames were cold and flickering with glamour, as false as the sidhe who conjured them.

They wouldn't dare attack at night, not while their prince was in residence and not while the Unseelie were strongest…

Unless they were ready to start a war.

CHAPTER SIX

The thought of war sent a cold chill through her. Balkin was down there somewhere, likely overseeing the contingent of demons Kal'thorz had sent as reinforcements. Sabine wasn't sure what her mother had promised the demon king, but it was likely something dear.

Sabine's gaze drifted toward the darkened forest and the trees that stood as steadfast sentinels. Her bedroom had one of the best views of the Silver Forest, second only to her mother's quarters on the upper level of the Winter Palace. The trees often whispered stories to her on nights like this one, but there was a strange feeling in the air tonight. They likely didn't care much for the fires burning along their border, even if they were fae-wrought.

The trees weren't truly silver. They were a deep, verdant green, their veins and trunks threaded with silver that shimmered through the branches. The silvery streaks reminded Sabine of her own markings, gleaming just as vividly against the paleness of her skin.

"As lovely as my markings are, yours are far more

astounding," Sabine said, allowing her words to carry on the wind to the trees. Their leaves rustled in pleasure. The Silver Trees were well-known for their vanity. Only fools would poke at the sentient trees—or burn Faerie fires at their edge.

The sound of a branch snapping caught her attention. Sabine scanned the ground close to the forest's edge but didn't see anything. Her skin prickled as though someone were watching her, but Sabine shook off her misgivings. It was likely an animal who was night-foraging. The Seelie couldn't have gotten past Balkin and the rest of the guards. Not with the demons patrolling the border.

An owl hooted in warning.

Sabine froze. Someone was out there, or the owl wouldn't have alerted her. The wards would prevent anyone with malice in their hearts from approaching, and no one would dare attempt to trespass her mother's personal boundaries without permission. There was another possibility, though.

Leaning out the window, Sabine called softly, "Averia? Is that you?"

There was no answer. If Averia hadn't received Sabine's letter in time, she might have gotten impatient and decided to sneak out. It wasn't the first time, but doing so now was risky.

Averia's family was as old as hers, but they were considered part of the lesser nobility. Queen Mali'theoria was content to suffer her daughter's friendship with Averia, but she wouldn't be amused by Averia slipping past her security measures. The imminent return of the Unseelie queen also meant there would be more guards than normal—and more chances to get caught.

Sabine paused, wondering if her friend even knew about the Seelie camped on their border. She quickly waved her hand, pulling back on her magic to dim the lanterns in her room. It took only a moment for her eyes to adjust to the darkness.

"You shouldn't be here," Sabine whispered into the night.

The leaves of the nearby trees rustled, but no one answered. Even the trees didn't respond.

She wasn't imagining it. Someone was out there. Another assassin? Sabine brushed her hair away from her face and glanced at the door. If she called for one of the guards and it was Averia, her friend would get into a mountain of trouble. Sabine didn't think any friendship could withstand being tortured.

If Balkin were here, she'd ask him to check. But her beastman protector wouldn't likely return until dawn. And despite his ambitions, not even Tarron would tempt her mother's wrath by disregarding orders.

A soft blue light pulsed at the edge of the forest. Sabine pressed her hands against the windowsill and leaned forward. It looked like a wisp.

Wisps danced with their own mysterious rhythm, flitting through the night like they were chasing forgotten laughter. But they rarely appeared alone. And this one… didn't move quite right.

It wasn't Averia. Her summoned lights were always violet. But there was one person whose magic mirrored that particular shade of blue.

A figure emerged from the shadows, cloaked in green and steeped in power so dense it clung to the darkness itself.

"Mother," Sabine whispered, both surprised she'd caught her return and wary of the circumstances. Queen Mali'theoria rarely traveled without her usual fanfare. For the Unseelie ruler to arrive alone, cloaked and silent, did not bode well.

Something must have gone wrong—either with the Council of Eight or with her negotiations with the Seelie. And there was only one Seelie of importance to both courts here tonight.

Rhys.

The blue light flickered once more, drifting between the trees. Sabine's stomach knotted. The last time Queen Mali'theoria had returned alone and cloaked, she'd sentenced a dozen members of the court to death. If she was meeting someone under the forest's cover tonight, it wasn't to exchange pleasantries.

And if those meetings had anything to do with the listening shard in her room—or her mother's plans for Rhys—then every hour she waited was another hour for the noose to tighten around him. He wouldn't see it coming. He wouldn't even know to fight. But she would. And she could.

She pressed her palms against the windowsill. Her mother wouldn't expect Sabine to follow. And if she was careful, no one else would see her.

Sabine turned from the window and slipped into the hall. It was empty. Her bare feet were silent against the polished wood, which warmed gently at her touch. She flicked her wrist to brighten one of the Faerie lanterns hovering in the corridor. The guards periodically patrolled these halls, but with Balkin away, they were likely stationed at the warded entrances to the royal quarters. Her tutor was another matter. Sabine had no desire to wake Giannia. She could be worse than a hungry orc when she didn't get enough sleep.

Rhys's chambers were across from her own, facing each

other like mirrors. She lowered his warding and eased open his door.

Shadows veiled the room. Moonlight filtered in, casting a faint glow across his sleeping form, and her heart ached at the sight of him. His features were so much like hers, from his silvery-white hair to the shape of his upturned nose. Only his eyes were different. Hers were a soft lavender, while his were a piercing blue.

Their father's eyes.

And more and more, his temperament.

Bitterness had taken root in Rhys, and she didn't know why it was growing so quickly. Perhaps it had started the day she'd been named heir, or maybe it began when her magic manifested and she required skin etchings—while his remained bare.

He'd always known he could never rule in the Unseelie court. His magic was too light, bound to the sun. The shadows would never claim him. But despite their mother's boasting, the sparkling throng of the Seelie court was no less brilliant or powerful than the Unseelie. Once his magic blossomed, he'd see that for himself.

Until then… Sabine bowed her head. The divide between them had already been forged. If there was danger, she would protect him. But if this was something else, it was a shadowed path she needed to walk alone—as an Unseelie.

Sabine swallowed and stepped back into the hallway, gently closing the door behind her.

She passed her tutor's room and entered the upper balcony hall. A tiny, wizened old woman with skin the color and texture of tree bark looked up at her. Unlike Sabine's pointed ears, the brownie's ears stuck out from her head like antennae. She grinned and rubbed her gnarled hands on her white apron.

The brownie leaned in and whispered, "Awake and up to mischief, eh, Princess? Need me to run interference for ya?"

Sabine shook her head and pressed her finger against her lips. "Just your silence, Mabla."

"Aye," Mabla nodded and thumped her chest. "I'll be keepin' the princess's secrets. 'Tis me honor. Shall I come back to clean later? Can't report anyone missin' if I don't see an empty bed."

Sabine smiled. "If you check back in a few hours, I'm sure I'll be in it."

"Then go, Princess, and step lightly. Tarron'ethos has been patrolling these halls this evening, and yer tutor's got ears sharp as the beastman," Mabla said, shooing her with enough enthusiasm to nearly shake her bun loose.

Sabine didn't need further encouragement. She darted down the hall toward the large balcony that overlooked the forest. In the distance, the blue glow of her mother's light still shimmered.

Eager to catch up, Sabine pressed her hand to the crystal railing and sent a trace of magic into it. The surface warmed beneath her touch, and the nearby silver tree responded, drawing one of the many lifts toward her.

She stepped inside and gripped the railing as the lift descended, her heart racing. Tonight, she would discover what secrets her mother had been hiding and do whatever was necessary to protect her brother.

No matter which court he claimed.

CHAPTER SEVEN

Sabine stepped off the lift, fumbling with her glamour. Pain flared along her left arm, the fresh mark burning like a brand and sending sharp pulses through her limbs. Gritting her teeth, she pushed through it, blurring her features and dimming the glow of her skin. It wasn't perfect, but it would hold.

Taking a deep breath, she raced toward the forest. The silver branches rustled overhead, echoing the pulse of magic still humming in the air. She pressed a hand to her chest, willing her heartbeat to slow as she listened for any sound of alarm. Fortunately, the guards were more concerned with keeping intruders out than tracking wayward daughters escaping into the trees.

Leaves crunched beneath her bare feet as she slipped farther into the forest, her nightgown whispering against her legs.

"Cover me," she whispered, trailing her fingers along the bark of a nearby silver tree. A slender vine with glowing threads curled down in response, brushing her ankle like a whisperfang seeking attention. The forest didn't speak in words, but it knew her. She'd spent more hours beneath these branches than within the palace walls.

Another breeze stirred the leaves, and the shadows thickened around her. Moss formed beneath her feet, silencing her footsteps. Up ahead, a flicker of her mother's light danced between the trunks.

It was still moving, drifting farther away. The cloaked figure flitted between the trees, encouraging her onward. Sabine quickened her pace, weaving through the roots and thorns with barely a sound. Branches bent aside as she passed, brushing her shoulders and parting like a veil. The Silver Forest was waking and responding to her presence.

The deeper she went, the colder the air became. Fog curled low to the ground, coiling around her feet like living smoke. The scent of nightbloom and ashvine filled her lungs, familiar, but sharper somehow.

Wrong.

She stopped at the edge of a clearing she didn't recognize, suddenly uneasy. She was well beyond the protective wards of the Winter Palace. The trees here grew farther apart, as if something had forced them back.

Instinct had her slipping behind one of the trunks. Something wasn't right.

The blue light hovered at the clearing's edge, pulsing once… then vanished. The echo of her mother's magic still shimmered in the air, but something about it rang hollow. It was little more than a reflection, not the source. It wasn't calling to her. It was *luring* her.

Sabine's breath caught as silence fell, so quiet, even the forest hushed. No wind. No rustle. No sound of insects or birds. Just the drum of her heartbeat and the sting of her mark. Magic clung to the air like ashfall.

She needed to turn back.

As she crept away from the tree, she caught sight of a

shape lying sprawled in the grass, half-obscured by fog. Something about the stillness of it chilled her. It looked like an animal—something broken and bleeding, barely breathing. Its aura was faint, barely glimmering in the moonlight. Her breath hitched. A green cloak lay crumpled on the ground, and beside it… a spill of silvery-white hair.

The silver crown at her mother's temple caught the moonlight, tarnished with blood.

"Mother?" she whispered in shocked horror.

Fingers clamped around her arm.

She gasped and instinctively jerked back. Giannia slammed her against the tree, one hand clamping tightly over Sabine's mouth, the other tightening on her freshly marked arm.

"Giannia?" Sabine's muffled voice broke beneath her palm.

"*Taciren*," Giannia whispered.

Agony exploded through Sabine as the word of power took hold. It seared into her skin, tore past her markings, and bound her from the inside out.

She couldn't move. Couldn't even cry out. The shock of betrayal lanced through her. It shouldn't be possible. Giannia was blood-sworn to her family's line.

Giannia's green eyes were wild, brimming with something Sabine couldn't name—fear, regret, resolve.

"She's passed beyond the Veil," Giannia whispered. "You can't help her now."

With a swift slash of her knife, she cut Sabine's palm and caught the blood in her hand. Giannia smeared it down Sabine's face, her whispered words spiraling into a strange, rhythmic cadence as she invoked her bloodline's magic.

"*Blood to bind, magic to veil. Her face I wear, her fate I trail.*"

Sabine's eyes widened in horror as Giannia smeared

the blood across her own skin. The world shimmered. Her vision blurred.

When it cleared, her tutor was gone. In her place stood a perfect copy of Sabine.

Giannia leaned in, her breath warm against Sabine's ear, "When the time comes, you must run, little star. One day, your magic will burn brighter than they ever imagined, and even the gods themselves will have to look away."

She unclasped the silver locket from around her neck. Sabine stared at the old heirloom in confusion. Giannia fastened it around Sabine's neck with shaking hands. The weight of the cold metal against her skin pressed just above her heart. The realization of what her tutor intended slammed into her.

With trembling fingers, Giannia pressed two fingers to Sabine's brow, lingering for one final heartbeat. Then she stepped back.

Sabine tried to shout, to stop her—but the silence was complete. The power word held her frozen against the tree, arms bound tight to her sides, her breath shallow in her chest. Even her tears refused to fall. She could only listen.

Blood dripped from her cut palm… The only part of her not bound by the magic.

Drip, drip, drip.

She willed it to fall faster, desperate to connect with the land. She couldn't let Giannia do this. Whatever had hurt her mother would destroy Giannia. Her tutor couldn't stand against such strength.

Giannia's footsteps drifted away, muffled by moss. Sabine reached for the threads that bound her blood to the forest.

The vines crept upward, coiling around Sabine's ankles.

Not tight. Not restraining. Protective. The forest was answering her call.

They slithered higher, brushing her calves, and winding around her thighs. A gentle tug pulled her backward. The bark behind her groaned softly as the tree shifted. A knot of roots surged from the base and nudged at her heels.

She slid down with a muted thud, her legs folding beneath her. No. This wasn't what she wanted. It had to break the magic. The vines hesitated, then wrapped tighter, cloaking her from sight. Sabine fought against the magical restraints. The damned trees were hiding her, not freeing her!

Only her eyes were left uncovered. From this angle, she could see beneath the mist and into the clearing beyond.

Her blood continued to fall in slow, rhythmic drops, soaking into the moss. The forest accepted it, the branches overhead rustling in response to her fear. Yet even then, the land refused to release her and continued to hold her in its protective embrace.

Giannia stepped into the clearing.

The mist parted.

At Giannia's feet, Queen Mali'theoria's body lay motionless amid the grass, her once-radiant gown darkened with blood.

Seelie guards, cloaked in golden light, emerged from the trees like phantoms. Their faces shifted and reformed —male, female, neither, both—flashing too quickly to focus. Sabine's heart raced. She couldn't tell how many there were. Ten? A dozen? More?

But she saw *him*.

King Cadan'ellesar—her father—stepped forward, his silhouette impossibly bright. He was an illusion of light and beauty that twisted something inside her. The others circled Giannia, their masks of glamour distorting their true selves. Magic pulsed like a sickness in the air.

Cadan lifted his hand. No warning. No words.

A bolt of magic speared toward Giannia.

She raised a shield just in time. It cracked beneath the force, splintering like ice. She staggered but held her ground.

"You think you can stand against our might?" a cloaked woman sneered, taking a step toward Giannia. "A mere *child?*"

Giannia remained silent, but kept her head held high. Glamour only affected sight. The moment she spoke, her identity would be revealed. Sabine fought against her restraints. Maybe if she could get free, they might have a chance.

Chains of light wrapped around Giannia's limbs. They yanked her to her knees as two fae advanced with cruel grins and blades drawn. They cut into her clothing, slicing away the soft fabric and digging into her skin. Magic whipped across Giannia's fair skin, slicing into her as her blood soaked the ground.

Giannia clamped her mouth shut, refusing to even cry out.

The others laughed and called out insults, their mocking voices infused with power. Even from this distance, Sabine could feel the weight of their magic shearing away at Giannia's resolve. Sabine strained against the magic binding her, against the vines' protective hold. Her blood dripped faster now, soaking into the moss like a prayer.

Two of the cloaked figures approached Giannia with dull metal chains held firmly in heavy gloves. Moving as one, they threw the chains over her.

The moment the metal touched her skin, she screamed.

The raw, ripping cry that tore from Giannia's throat shattered Sabine's thoughts, splintering through her like breaking glass. Giannia's glamour fractured. The illusion of Sabine dissolved, leaving her tutor's true form crumpled atop Sabine's mother, her skin blistered and bleeding where the chains clawed into her.

"A trick," Cadan snarled, taking a threatening step toward her. "Where is your charge?"

Giannia lifted her head and ground out, "Her path is written in the bark and bone of this forest. Even your light can't erase that."

One of the fae stepped forward, his sword drawn. As though Giannia were nothing more than a nuisance to be brushed aside, he ran his blade through her heart. She let out a choked gasp and fell to the ground.

"*Balkin!*" Sabine screamed soundlessly, the mental call ripping across her psyche. The trees around them trembled, their branches shuddering from the force of her mental shout.

Cadan lifted his head, his gaze sweeping the clearing, his expression murderous. He snapped his fingers at his companions. "Find her! She's here in the forest. I want her lifeblood soaking the ground before dawn's embrace."

Sabine didn't breathe. Didn't dare move. The vines tightened, and the forest held its breath with her.

Beneath the moss, her blood still flowed.

And the land listened.

CHAPTER EIGHT

A tremor rippled through the roots.

Far off, a roar cracked the silence.

And then… screams.

The air exploded with chaos. Magic tore through the trees in jagged bursts of light. From the eastern border where the Seelie fires burned, a wall of Unseelie shadows surged forward—demon flame colliding with golden light in a storm of fury.

Sabine barely had time to register the distant clash before the vines unspooled from her limbs and the magic holding her snapped.

She scrambled across the ground with a gasp, breathing in air that burned like smoke. Her arms shook as she pushed herself up. The forest was moving, guiding her. A root lifted beneath her hand. Another braced her side.

And then… he was there.

Balkin burst through the mist in his lion form, his golden eyes blazing with fury. For an instant she thought she was hallucinating, then his roar shattered the illusion.

Blood streaked his mane, a jagged tear splitting one ear.

He must have torn through the warded forest paths in minutes to reach her.

"Get up! Now!"

His mental shout sliced through her shock. Sabine staggered to her feet. She made it two steps before faltering.

"No—my mother. Giannia—"

"Gone," Balkin said with a growl. *"You cannot help them. But you can live. Now ride!"*

She bit back a sob and scrambled onto his back, wrapping her arms around his neck and curling into his thick mane. He leaped forward, paws pounding the moss, dodging twisted roots and shattered magic.

Behind them, the clash of weapons grew louder, the forest howled—but the sound deepened, ancient, older than war. Sparks of Seelie gold and Unseelie black fire lit the mist ahead, then everything went black.

The land answered.

Darkness spilled out between the trees, not like shadow, but like something alive. The air tasted of metal and rot, thick with the weight of old oaths. A writhing mass of teeth and antlers and smoke, racing the wind itself. The ground iced beneath their hooves. Bark split open. The forest recoiled from their passing—as if even the ancient trees feared what they once served.

The Wild Hunt.

Sabine clung to Balkin's back, her cheek pressed to his fur. The wind stung her eyes, but she didn't dare blink. Twisted faces flashed past, hounds with molten eyes, riders cloaked in bone, a stag-headed creature wreathed in fire. Creatures of nightmare swept past her, circling, howling.

"Hold."

The mental command rang through her like a crashing cymbal. Balkin's feet locked, and he skidded to a halt. Sabine tumbled from his back and landed in a crumpled heap. Around them, the Hunt circled tighter, drawing in like a noose.

She was going to die in this forest.

Like her mother.

Like Giannia.

At the center of the writhing mass of nightmares, something stepped from the shadows. He was taller than any man, antlered, crowned in thorns and starlight. His antlers rose high above him, bone white and glistening, while shadows clung to the tattered edges of his cloak. His glowing red eyes fell upon her, the stark white of his skeletal hands grasping an ancient, withered staff.

The Huntsman.

His presence was a void, sucking the light from the air, warping the trees and silencing the wind. Even the forest dared not breathe.

Balkin growled low in his throat. *"Keep your silence, Sabin'theoria."*

Sabine swallowed, her entire body trembling. She wasn't sure she *could* speak, even if she wanted to.

The beastman rose, his fur rippling as his lion's bulk folded inward, bones reshaping until he stood upright on two legs. Golden hair framed his muzzle like a mane, and his whiskers twitched with restrained fury as words rumbled from his elongated snout. "She is not ready to assume the throne."

The Huntsman's fiery gaze seared into her, as if he could rip the secrets from her very soul. Her breath hitched. Her fingers curled into the soil.

The Huntsman's ancient voice echoed in her thoughts, strangely hypnotic and achingly familiar. *"The Hunt does not wait on readiness. It answers prophecy. Rights of blood must be satisfied."*

Sabine tried to speak, but the words died on her

tongue. Something pressed down on her chest like stone. Her pulse pounded in her ears. She could *feel* them watching—every hound, every rider. If she moved wrong, they would descend.

What sort of sidhe cowered in the dirt, unable to even speak?

And they expected her to be queen?

Balkin growled again and took a step forward. "If you force her to claim her birthright now, you will be sentencing her to death."

The Huntsman studied her for a long, terrible moment. She could feel him weighing and judging her—leaves strewn through her silvery hair, her nightgown spattered with blood and dirt. Even the natural glow of her skin was muted, as though it had forgotten how to shine.

It was her mother who was queen, not her. This was all a terrible mistake.

"The land has claimed her."

Sabine bit back a hysterical laugh. To the underworld with that. The godsforsaken land had abandoned her family and her friend. A sob gathered in her throat.

Branches above them twisted. The moss trembled.

"But the Hunt will wait... once. Speak your vow."

Sabine blinked, disoriented by the sudden stillness. She didn't understand until Balkin dropped to one knee, reaching for her bleeding hand.

"She will return to Faerie and take her rightful place. I swear it by tooth and claw, by mark and blood."

Silence.

The Huntsman lifted a skeletal hand.

The Hunt withdrew as one, melting into the forest like mist.

His gaze fell on Sabine one last time. *"Then see that she lives."*

And he vanished.

For a long moment, only the echo of hoofbeats remained. Then even that was gone.

Sabine lay in the dirt, her body trembling from exertion and fear. The air was still thick with the Hunt's magic—dense and clinging, like ash soaked in blood. She couldn't move. Could barely think.

She choked back a sob.

Balkin kneeled beside her, claws retracted, golden eyes scanning the trees. "We must go, my darling kitten. The Seelie will be here any moment."

Sabine didn't answer. She couldn't. Her gaze was still fixed on the spot where the Huntsman had stood. Even now, the shadows there seemed deeper, like the memory of him had sunk into the roots and refused to leave.

None of this was real. Her mother had to still be alive. Queen Mali'theoria was the most powerful Unseelie ruler in generations.

It must be a Seelie trick. Her father could never have gathered enough power to murder her mother under the cover of night, not while her magic was strongest.

Had the Seelie found some new claim to the darkness she didn't know about? Or was it some other treachery entirely?

And yet... the image of the broken figure in the forest clearing was seared into her thoughts.

A branch cracked in the distance.

Seelie scouts.

Balkin hauled her to her feet. "There is no time to mourn. We must be away before the Seelie strike."

"I watched them die," she whispered.

"I know." His voice was gruff, but there was something gentler beneath it. "But you will not join them tonight."

The wind shifted. Magic still scorched the air, but

something older stirred beneath it. The silver trees began to hum again, low and mournful.

"My father won't stop hunting me, will he?" Sabine pressed a hand to her chest, feeling the hollow ache blooming inside. All the assassination attempts. All the death. It was too much. "He'll never stop until I'm dead."

"No," Balkin said. "But we have allies. Come."

He dropped to all fours and shifted into his lion form.

Taking a shaky breath, Sabine climbed onto his back once more. This time, she didn't cling out of panic. She gripped the thick fur around his neck like a lifeline—because it was.

Balkin surged into motion, and the forest parted before them. The wind tore at her hair, carrying the scent of blood and ash.

She didn't look back. She couldn't. Behind them, the forest closed over the dead, burying the night's horrors beneath its roots while the sound of battle in the distance echoed behind them.

The only way to survive now was to find the strength to rule.

CHAPTER NINE

The night had turned cold by the time they reached the outskirts of one of the beastpeople's villages.

Balkin kept to the shadows, his golden eyes flicking between the dense tree cover and the narrow, half-overgrown path. Sabine clung to his back, half-conscious and shivering, the faint metallic scent of dried blood lingering like a memory she couldn't shake.

The forest around them had quieted, but the silence wasn't comforting. It was heavy, like the land itself was holding its breath.

They bypassed the main cluster of huts entirely. Balkin's village was dark and still, nestled in the roots of the ancient silverwood trees. She'd only been here a handful of times when she was younger, and not for many years.

Instead, Balkin veered left, padding down a narrow trail worn into the moss. The path twisted between the gnarled roots, deeper into the forest, until a low stone dwelling came into view, half-grown into the base of an enormous hollowed trunk.

A soft light flickered within.

Balkin lowered himself to the ground, and Sabine carefully slid off his back. She threaded her fingers through his thick mane, unwilling to release him just yet. Her knees were still shaky.

The door creaked open before they reached it, revealing the dim silhouette of a small, hunched figure draped in feathers and beads. Pale, luminous eyes blinked slowly in the dark.

"About time," Usagi said, her voice dry as the wind over fallen leaves. "Bring her in. Make sure you wipe your paws first."

Balkin chuffed but obeyed, nudging Sabine inside with his furry head.

The air smelled of cedar, ash, and something sweet and overripe, like plums left too long in the sun. Bundles of herbs in various stages of drying dangled from the rafters. The space was cramped but warm, lined with old furs and nest-like piles of feathers, dried grasses, and sheared wool.

A dozen pairs of owl-shaped eyes stared at Sabine from carvings, masks, and polished stones, each one positioned as though watching the hut's occupants. Sabine had spent several quiet afternoons here, watching Usagi carve stones with her talons while recounting tales of beastpeople heroes long forgotten by most of Faerie.

Usagi's clawed feet scraped quietly against the stone floor. Her feathers weren't merely decorative. Patches of mottled brown and silver-gray covered her shoulders and extended halfway down her arms. Tufts of down puffed slightly whenever she breathed.

She reached out a feathered hand and brushed Sabine's cheek with a single claw.

"So much blood," she murmured, her voice almost too soft to catch. "And none of it the worst that's to come."

Sabine swayed, suddenly dizzy. She clasped the locket around her neck like a lifeline.

"Sit," Usagi squawked, already moving to clear a pile of parchments and broken crystals from a short stump beside the fire. "And no collapsing on the floor. You're not dead yet."

Balkin gave a low rumble of amusement and padded to the back wall. A small storage shelf held almost a dozen wrapped satchels. He nosed one open and gingerly lifted it between his teeth, careful enough that Sabine heard only the faint clink of glass inside. He set it aside and reached for another. She caught a brief glimpse of folded cloth, perhaps a cloak or clothing, before it disappeared beneath his massive paws.

Sabine sank onto the stump and wrapped her arms around herself. Balkin had planned for this. Of course he had. Usagi had probably given him warning years ago.

She opened her mouth to speak and then closed it again. If this had been foreseen, why hadn't they warned her mother?

Usagi waddled to the small stove and poured steaming water from a kettle into a clay cup. Lifting it with her feathered hands, she turned her glowing gaze back to Sabine. "You don't remember the dreams, do you? Not yet. But you will. They always come."

Sabine accepted the cup, wrapping her hands around its warmth. "Dreams?"

Usagi clicked her beak, a sound halfway between a tsk and a chime. "Ah. So the forest hasn't told you everything. Good. It's better that way. If you knew the shape of the ending, you might try to change it. And we can't have that."

Sabine opened her mouth to protest, but Usagi waved a

feathered hand and turned away. "You'd best not be making a mess, Balkin Lioneyes. I'm watching you. I don't want to be picking lion hair out of my beak for the next week."

Balkin let out a low, complaining growl.

Usagi muttered to herself as she tidied a cluttered shelf. "The stars are out of order, and the crows are watching the moon again. Nothing good comes of that. Faerie queens drenched in blood. A golden child on my doorstep."

Sabine glanced at Balkin, her fingers tightening on the cup. She wouldn't dare drink one of Usagi's concoctions, not until Balkin confirmed it was safe.

"Tell me what's going on," she said, her voice hoarse. "Did my father—why did he kill them?"

Balkin shifted into his humanoid form. Sabine frowned. Here, in their home village, they preferred staying in their animal forms. Too many shifts in such a short amount of time would strain his magic, but hands were better suited to handling delicate items.

He lifted one of the glass bottles, sniffed at it, then wrapped it in soft fabric and placed it into a larger bag. "Rhys has not yet renounced his ties to the Unseelie."

Sabine's brow furrowed. "The ceremony is tomorr—"

Her voice broke. The tea sloshed over the cup's rim. Usagi swooped in and whisked it away with a squawk, muttering as she dabbed the floor with a cloth.

Rhys wouldn't be renouncing his ties. As the Unseelie heir, Sabine would have to be the one to conduct the ceremony.

Sabine swallowed, her hands curling into fists in her lap. "You think they're attempting a coup?"

"Yes, my darling kitten," Balkin said. "The Seelie guards didn't stumble onto the Winter Palace's lands by accident. They crossed the wards without resistance. Someone either took them down from the inside... or invited them in."

Usagi's feathers fluffed in agitation. "Traitors in your mother's court? Tch. That nest's been rotting for years."

Sabine shook her head. "Rhys wouldn't have taken part in any plots that could harm our mother."

Her voice faltered. Oh, gods. Rhys didn't know.

"I need to tell him," she whispered.

Balkin snarled. "You will do no such thing."

She stood on shaking legs. "He shouldn't hear this from the Council. Or the guards. He needs to know what our father's done!"

"Your enemies will be watching the Winter Palace," Balkin said. "Every move from here must be planned carefully. Your survival is paramount."

"But—"

Balkin put his hands on her shoulders and lowered her back down on the stool. "No one has more to gain from your mother's death than her heir."

Sabine flinched. "I didn't—"

Usagi clicked her beak. "We know, child."

When Sabine made no move to get up again, Balkin growled low in approval and continued packing supplies. "The Seelie King has wanted you gone since the day you were born. Either dead by his hand, or sentenced to such for murdering the queen."

Sabine's pulse roared in her ears, and she shook her head. The assassination attempts. Her mother's restrictions. Even as a child, she'd known King Cadan hated her. But the Council had paired Queen Mali'theoria and King Cadan'ellesar together, believing their union would be the magical catalyst needed to breathe new life into the courts.

It had worked. Their coupling had resulted in not just one child, but twins. The Council had declared the feat miraculous, and the people had rejoiced. The fae had never been prolific, but ever since the Dragon War, it had become more difficult to reproduce.

"Why?" she whispered. "I'm no threat to him."

Balkin turned to face her fully, his golden gaze burning. "He has feared you from the beginning, kitten. You carry both sides of the Court's magic, light and dark. You were always going to be a threat to him and to Rhys. The question was when."

Usagi turned, folding her arms across her feathered chest. "The stars whispered of betrayal long before you drew breath. Blood begets blood. You can't remain in Faerie now. Not without a war. And not unless you're ready to end one."

Sabine's thoughts reeled. This had to be some terrible mistake. The Council would intervene. There were laws. Rituals. Balance.

But that was the student talking. The daughter. The truth was never so neat, and her mother never would have tolerated Sabine showing such weakness. And Giannia had died to protect her.

"Neither Rhys nor I are strong enough to rule yet," Sabine said, shaking her head. "The Council of Eight won't install a Seelie King to act as regent for the Unseelie throne. None of this makes sense. Why now?"

"Because the time has come," Usagi said, solemn and soft. "And your name is no longer just a name. It's a prophecy."

Usagi's ramblings were always confusing and jumbled with ominous foretellings and random thoughts.

Sabine looked to Balkin, her breath catching. "What do we do?"

Balkin padded forward and placed his clawed hand on her shoulder. "You leave Faerie. I'll take you to a place where the Seelie can't reach you. Where even the Council won't think to look. You'll learn to survive. To fight. To hide who you are until you're strong enough to claim your birthright with blood and magic."

She jerked back in shock. Leave Faerie? Her home?

This was all she'd ever known. No one left Faerie, not unless they'd committed a crime so heinous that even the land turned away from them. Leaving Faerie would be like leaving a part of herself behind. She couldn't do that…

The silver trees had always sung to her; tonight, they only shivered. Even the land seemed to mourn her, not claim her.

And yet, if she stayed, she would die.

Giannia's final words echoed in her mind: *When the time comes, you must run, little star. One day, your magic will burn brighter than they ever imagined—and even the gods themselves will have to look away.*

Sabine's voice cracked. "How long?"

Usagi's eyes gleamed like twin moons. "Until the Hunt rides again. Until the forest burns. When the lost heir returns with fire in her hands and ash at her heels, and dragons streak across the night sky."

Sabine shivered.

Balkin picked up the cup, sniffed it, then handed it to her with a nod.

Sabine stared down into the contents, the warm liquid now gone cold. She took a sip of the bitter brew.

"I don't want this," she whispered, unsure whether she meant the tea or her fate.

"No," Balkin said softly. "But there is no acceptable alternative."

The ancient woman crouched beside the fire, her owl-shaped eyes reflecting its flame. "Dawn's not far. The Hunt is hungry, and the Seelie still sniff the trees like wolves that lost the scent. They shall descend upon our village at first light."

Balkin slung the satchels over his shoulder. "We'll use the old path. Through the root tunnels."

Rising in a rustle of feathers and bones, the woman motioned to the tea in Sabine's hand. "Drink it all, little sapling. You'll need your strength."

She drained the cup, her legs trembling as she stood. "Where are we going?"

"Somewhere you can disappear. Until you're strong enough to return."

Sabine looked away, but Usagi tilted her head and whispered, "You don't have to want it yet. You just have to live."

Usagi lifted a cloak from a hanging peg and wrapped it around Sabine. She smoothed it around Sabine's shoulders, her clawed thumb brushing along the seam. "You were born for the between places, child. Not of Seelie. Not of Unseelie. Not yet queen. Not yet free."

Outside, the wind shifted, and a long, low howl cut through the trees.

Balkin turned to the door. "It's time."

Sabine threw her arms around the older beastwoman. Usagi stroked her hair once, then reached up to a crowded shelf and pressed something smooth and cool into her hand.

A polished stone. Carved with a tiny owl.

"I will watch over you," Usagi said, her voice solemn. "Now fly, little bird. Fly and be free."

Sabine swallowed, her hand curling tight around the charm. Then she followed Balkin into the dark.

CHAPTER TEN

Dawn crept over the treetops.

Sabine clung to Balkin's back, her fingers tangled in his mane, her body aching from the long ride. The once-familiar trees had thinned, giving way to brambles and rougher terrain. The forest no longer embraced her. Its silence was too still, too strained—like something sacred had been broken and the land hadn't yet decided whether to mourn or rage.

They'd passed beyond the boundaries of Faerie hours ago.

She didn't ask where they were going. She didn't have the strength. Her thoughts floated just out of reach, like half-formed dreams. Whatever vitality had been brewed in Usagi's tea had long since fled.

If she'd stayed within the palace, Giannia might still be alive. If she'd only spoken to Tarron, the guards might have arrived in the clearing soon enough to save her mother. Dozens of scenarios floated through her thoughts. The scent of blood still clinging to her skin was a constant reminder of her loss.

They crested a low rise and descended toward a shallow hollow. Tucked beneath a natural ridge and mostly hidden behind a screen of wind-stunted trees was a small cottage, no larger than a hunter's den.

Sabine wrinkled her nose. No wonder the forest was offended. It was human-built, by the look of the rudimentary stonework. The kind of place that wore its edges blunt and ugly, a desecration of the beauty and balance found in nature.

The air was sharper here, tinged with salt from the sea and something fouler. Coal smoke, maybe? A city or village had to be nearby.

"No," she said, her fingers tightening in Balkin's mane. "You cannot expect me to hide here, surrounded by dead wood and stone."

Balkin's mind touched hers. *It will be temporary. You must embrace the illusion of being human. This shall be your school. You will learn to speak, act, and behave as a human. It is the only way to ensure the Seelie won't discover you.*

Sabine clenched her jaw. Her common tongue was passable in theory, but like most fae, she struggled to make certain sounds. It was a flat language, without the nuance and melody the fae infused into their words.

She didn't know anything about humans. She'd glimpsed a few changelings that were brought to the court, but the sidhe didn't interact with them. They were a novelty, a distraction. Not something to aspire to.

"I've arranged for teachers to aid you," Balkin said, continuing to pad toward the cottage door. *"Two demons will guide you in controlling and concealing your magic, while the witch will help you perfect your human glamour and show you how to blend into the human world. They should arrive soon."*

Sabine exhaled sharply. "Demons?"

"Exiles from Kal'thorz's realm," Balkin explained. *"They are*

among the fiercest of the underworld's warriors and were carefully chosen for this purpose. They will protect you until you're strong enough to claim your throne."

She didn't trust demons. Her mother and Kal'thorz had been enmeshed in a battle of wills for centuries. They were part of the Unseelie court, but their loyalty belonged only to those who proved themselves stronger.

If Sabine slipped, even for a moment, she would become nothing more than a puppet.

Balkin stopped in front of the cottage door and lowered himself to the ground. She slid off his back and removed the satchels, waiting for him to transform.

Once he'd shifted, Balkin took the satchels and opened the door for her, gesturing her inside.

The cottage was small, dark, and smelled faintly of soot and something fermented. Sabine stood just inside the threshold, unmoving, her hand still pressed to the dead, wooden doorframe. Sunlight spilled in behind her, illuminating the warped floorboards on the porch, but the shadows inside felt heavy and alive.

She took a tentative step forward, the rough floor creaking beneath her bare feet. A cobweb brushed her cheek. She absently flicked it away and summoned a light source in her palm.

"No magic," Balkin said sharply from behind her.

"No... magic?" she whispered, the glow fizzling at her fingertips. She forced her hand back to her side, swallowing hard as Balkin stepped around her. He pulled a glass lantern from the shelf and handed it to her.

The glass contraption reeked faintly of oil. Balkin lifted the cover and struck what looked like two rocks together, sending a spark flying upon a thin strip of fabric.

It caught fire, and she nearly dropped it. She thrust it toward him and stepped backward, fingers trembling.

"Isn't it dangerous to have such a thing here?" Sabine asked, eyeing the strange lantern with trepidation. "If the trees that formed this cottage were still living, they would have already evicted us."

Balkin chuckled and hung the lantern from a ceiling peg. "This is how humans see at night. You'll need to get used to it."

Sabine scooted around the lantern, giving it a wide berth. A single wooden table sat beneath a crooked beam. A narrow fireplace took up the far wall, blackened with old soot. A rickety staircase climbed into darkness. Bundles of dried herbs dangled from the rafters, giving the place a sharp, astringent scent that clung to her throat.

This wasn't a sanctuary. It was a cage of stone and smoke.

She moved deeper inside, trailing her fingers along the edge of the table. Dust coated the surface, and she resisted the urge to clean it with a flick of magic. Even that small act could get her caught.

Balkin closed the door with a quiet thud and dropped the satchels on the table. "This cottage is warded, along with the perimeter. No one will sense you here. But we must remain vigilant."

"Where are the brownies?" she asked, wondering how humans could live in such surroundings. "Did the humans neglect to leave them offerings?"

"No," he said. "This place was abandoned long ago. The witch will show you how to care for it in the way of humans. We could not risk exposing more of our plan to outsiders."

Sabine's heart gave a little flutter of panic. She didn't know how to cook. She didn't know how to clean. She didn't even know how to start a fire without magic.

She sank onto the edge of a narrow wooden bench

beside the hearth and hugged her arms around her knees. The floor was cold beneath her feet, the silence oppressive.

Without her magic, she was nothing.

"I don't know how to do this."

"No," Balkin said, his golden eyes glinting in the dim light. "But you will learn."

Balkin took down a second lantern from a hook by the hearth. He sat beside her and said, "Open the glass panel to expose the wick."

She lifted the latch, and the small door creaked open. Balkin handed her a small striker and a piece of flint.

"Strike them together until the spark catches the wick," he said. "The lantern burns oil," he added. "Humans use it instead of summoning a light source."

Sabine studied the items with a frown. "How did humans learn to trap fire in stones?"

"Humans are both industrious and resilient, my darling kitten," Balkin said with a smile. "You will learn to be, as well."

Sabine struck the stones together. Nothing happened. She tried again, and a spark flickered to the ground. More confident now, she leaned forward and struck them together again. A spark caught, and the fire leapt to life. For the first time since the forest, something small obeyed her will. The faintest smile tugged at her lips before fading.

He closed the panel and offered it to her. She took it gingerly, holding it away from her body. The lifeless wood surrounding them might be unaware of the potential for destruction, but Sabine couldn't quite bridge that hurdle yet.

"You can go upstairs to freshen up," Balkin said, rising to his feet. "I need to check the perimeter wards before our guests arrive. They'll be bringing the rest of the supplies."

He paused. "The Council will assume you're dead by

now. Tarron'ethos will delay the reports as long as he can. Preventing your guard from seeking you out will be the real challenge, I suspect." Balkin rubbed his chin. "A few still loyal to you will feed us information from the Winter Palace."

Sabine lifted her head. "Loyal to me? Or to my mother's throne?"

Balkin's whiskers twitched. "In Faerie, the difference is a matter of convenience."

Sabine wanted to argue, but he was right. Loyalty in Faerie was always a transaction.

She turned back to study the lantern and asked, "How long will it burn?"

"Several hours, until you need to refill it," Balkin said as he pulled the door open. "Don't set yourself on fire. And don't use magic."

She shot him an exasperated look, but he was already gone.

She swept her gaze over the room again. So this was what it meant to be human: to survive without magic, without melody, without the forest's song.

Sabine looked up at the steep staircase. The steps were uneven, and the railing was just a rope, tied loosely between wooden pegs. She made her way up slowly, her bare feet brushing dust from each stair. At the top, the space opened into a cramped loft with slanted rafters and a low-beamed ceiling.

A small washstand stood beside the far window. A tarnished mirror hung above a wide ceramic basin, its surface dry and cracked from age. A wooden pump was mounted into the wall beside it.

Sabine eyed it warily.

She set the lantern on the edge of the washstand, then grasped the pump's handle and tried pulling it upward.

Nothing happened. She pushed. Still nothing. She glared at it, then gave it a more forceful jerk. It groaned once, and then finally coughed up a sputter of brownish water, followed by a thin stream of cold, clear liquid.

Sabine let it run for a moment before filling the basin.

The water was shockingly cold. She gasped as she dipped her fingers in, then used the frayed cloth beside it to scrub at the blood staining her hands and arms. Her nightgown clung damply to her skin, the once silky material now streaked with filth and dried sap.

Her hair had come loose from its braid, the silvery strands tangled and snarled. She worked her fingers through the worst of the knots with an almost desperate need to find some order in the chaos. A snag caught on twigs and dried blood, and she bit the inside of her cheek to keep from crying out.

She didn't recognize the girl in the mirror. Her cheeks were hollowed from exhaustion, her eyes shadowed with grief. The golden vine-like pattern of her newly etched magical mark shimmered faintly beneath her skin, pulsing with restrained power. But even that light seemed distant now, dulled beneath the weight of everything she'd lost. Giannia's locket hung heavily on her chest, carrying a weight she couldn't bear.

She sank to the floor, tucking her knees to her chest. Her cloak slipped from her shoulders and pooled beside her on the floor. She wrapped her hand around the locket, and her eyes welled with tears.

The silence pressed in again, thicker than before. In Faerie, even silence had a melody—a rhythm shaped by wind through leaves, the hum of magic in the air, the laughter of unseen spirits. Here, it was just… empty.

Like her.

A faint tremor rippled through the warding lines

outside, the kind that came when other magic brushed against it. Footsteps crunched softly outside the cottage. Sabine stiffened.

The front door creaked open.

"You're late," Balkin said, using the same tone he often did with the guards.

"You said dawn," a deeper voice rumbled, the arrogance and richness of the sound strangely appealing.

A woman's soft and lilting response followed, too low to hear. But the warmth of her voice, threaded with the unmistakable shimmer of familiar magic, was a touch of home.

Sabine wiped her eyes and rose, drawn toward the sound. She crossed to the top of the stairs, the lantern's light flickering against the walls.

She didn't descend. Not yet. She caught a glimpse of midnight skin, silver horns, and red hair.

The demons and the witch had arrived.

CHAPTER ELEVEN

Sabine quickly splashed cold water on her face, wincing as it stung the scrapes along her jaw and hairline. Her reflection wavered in the tarnished mirror, a far cry from the regal poise she once wore like a second skin.

She couldn't even use glamour to hide the shadows beneath her eyes, proof of how far she'd fallen.

Bracing her palms against the basin's edge, she forced herself to breathe.

They will not see weakness.

She lifted her head in determination. She pinched her cheeks until color bloomed beneath her fingertips, then dragged her fingers through her damp hair, twisting the tangled strands into something resembling order.

She was sidhe. Even stripped of court and crown, she would act like it.

Lantern in hand, she descended the creaking staircase with slow, measured steps. The three strangers turned toward her.

Two of the largest demons she'd ever seen stood near

the fireplace. They were both tall and broad, with obsidian-toned skin that shimmered like polished stone. Horns curled from their temples, sweeping back over their bald heads.

The first had his arms crossed over his chest, a faint smirk tugging at the edge of his mouth. Yet his gaze was heated as he slowly perused her body, the thin material of her nightgown doing little for modesty's sake.

Still, she kept her head high and held his gaze. Her pride demanded it, though something in his look sparked an answering heat she refused to acknowledge. Hunger flickered across his features, answered by something deep within her. She'd met other demons, but none had ever drawn her like this. Her Unseelie magic stirred, unbidden, as if sensing and responding to the darkness within him.

Not good.

Balkin gestured to him and said, "Allow me to introduce Dax'than Versed. And his brother, Bane'umbra."

Sabine's eyes sharpened on Balkin. "Versed?"

Dax took a step toward her and gave a mocking bow. "A pity your beastman protector didn't warn you that you'd be entertaining two demon princes." His amber gaze roamed over her again, lingering on the thin fabric clinging to her curves until her skin pebbled in awareness. "I prefer my lessons hands-on, *Your Highness*. And I assure you—they tend to leave a mark." He moved closer, his lips curving in a wicked smile. "Shall we begin?"

Fury slammed into her at his insinuation. She flicked her wrist, flinging Dax against the wall. A bottle teetered on the table and crashed to the ground, shattering into pieces.

Balkin's snarl ripped through the room as he surged forward and slammed Dax against the wall before he could recover. The floor groaned beneath the force of the impact, dust drifting from the rafters.

The second demon simply crossed his arms, his gaze fixed on her with thoughtful intensity. The woman Sabine had scarcely noticed before, whose magic had felt almost familiar, stood several steps away from the demons.

Her hair was a riot of red curls that caught the light like fire, and her colorful skirts swished in a blur of rainbow hues. Her mouth curved in an amused grin, and her green eyes sparkled with humor. There was an earthy vitality about the woman that Sabine found strangely fascinating.

"If we were still in Faerie, you would be on the ground, begging for her forgiveness," Balkin growled, his voice low and dangerous. "You were told to train her, not provoke her. She is a Faerie royal, the last of her mother's line, and heir to the Unseelie throne. If you do not give her the respect she is due, I will end you."

Dax's eyes flashed silver in challenge, even as Balkin's clawed hand tightened around his throat. Sabine's pulse hammered, the urge to stop them warring with the sting of her own humiliation. Balkin had warned her against using magic. She'd already lost control, and now her protector was cleaning up the mess she'd made.

Her jaw clenched. She turned on her heel and walked out the cottage door, unable to stand there a minute longer.

Cool air hit her as she stepped outside, but it did nothing to steady her.

It wasn't the demon's fault. It was hers. Her first test, and she'd already failed. Balkin had chosen the demon king's sons to teach her control in the most profound way. But she wasn't sure she was up to the challenge.

She headed through a small, derelict garden and into a wooded area behind the cabin. The perimeter wards thrummed against her magic, barring escape. Even here, she was trapped, unable to take a single step beyond the boundary to breathe.

She pressed her hands against a tree, the rough bark offering little comfort. Everything here was dulled, the land scarcely recognized her. She stared up at the tree, battling her desire to infuse her magic into it.

Soft footsteps crunched on the leaves behind her.

"I would've turned him into a frog," a woman said, a trace of humor in her voice. "But flinging him into the wall was a solid choice. Nice technique."

Sabine frowned and ran her hand over the trunk. "I wasn't aiming to impress."

"No, but you certainly got the room's attention." A beat passed. "I'm Esme, by the way."

Sabine turned. The woman from earlier stood a few paces away, watching her with mild amusement. Her curls glinted copper in the morning light, and there was a knowing sparkle in her green eyes.

She found herself strangely fascinated. Among the sidhe, hair was always straight and fine. Esme's striking curls looked like they'd spring back if touched. She was oddly tempted to try.

"Your name is Esme?" Sabine asked instead, uncertain of the social etiquette when dealing with a human. If this witch were sidhe, she would have waited to address Sabine until she had finished communing with the tree. Interrupting was… rude. It simply wasn't done. No wonder the trees were more comfortable ignoring humans.

"Well, it's actually Esmelle. But we won't get into the teasing jokes I endured for years in the orphanage. No idea what they'd been thinking naming me something that rhymed with 'smell'."

Sabine tilted her head, puzzled. "What is an... orphanage?"

Esme made a sound somewhere between a laugh and a groan. She picked up a stick from the ground and twirled it between her fingers. "Wow, okay. This is going to be more challenging than I thought."

Sabine watched her warily. "Why?"

"Because you don't know anything about humans. Which makes sense. I don't know much about the fae either, except for crazy stories about powerful magic strong enough to bend the elements. But that also means we're starting from the very beginning." She jabbed the stick in the dirt. "An orphanage is where human children live if they don't have parents or anyone to take care of them. Some end up on the streets when no one comes for them."

Sabine stared at her in horror. "Humans... abandon their young?"

Esme paused, a brow creasing her forehead. "Fae are different?"

"Children are precious and rare," Sabine said, her magic flaring to the surface as anger took hold. "If there was a child without a home, one would be found—or they would be cared for by the monarch where they lived. They would *never* be abandoned."

Esme was silent a moment, then nodded slowly. "That's... kind of beautiful, actually."

Sabine frowned. "It's expected."

"Well, if it helps, not all humans are monsters," Esme said lightly. "Some of us even like kids. Or at least the idea of them." She offered a small smile. "I never had any family, so I guess I learned early how to take care of myself."

Sabine glanced back at the cottage, the ugly and odd

little building still visible through the trees. "Balkin said you intended to teach me how to act human."

Esme nodded. "Yeah. In exchange, the dark and broody brothers promised you'd teach me about my magic."

Sabine's gaze flew back to her. "You don't know how to use magic?"

Esme gave her a sheepish look. "Not exactly. Being surrounded by humans made it difficult to learn. Dax and Bane said I'm part-dryad. I've always had a knack for growing things, but there's always been something missing."

Sabine held out her hand. Esme regarded her with surprise but placed her hand in Sabine's outstretched one. Sabine guided her down beside the stick protruding from the earth and said, "Wrap your hand around it."

Esme did as she was told, and Sabine reached for the essence of the tree. A faint flicker of awareness touched her thoughts, warm and green as spring.

"I feel it," Esme breathed, her green eyes wide.

"Call to it," Sabine said softly. "Gently encourage it to grow. Reach into the soil with your thoughts and feel where the roots want to take hold. Let them form, then guide the stem upward toward the sun for strength."

The stick trembled beneath their joined hands. Tiny green shoots sprouted at the base, leaves unfurling like sleeping wings.

Esme let out a quiet gasp. "That was me?"

"The magic within you was already there," Sabine said, releasing her grip. "I simply showed you how to guide it."

Esme stared at the new growth as though it were a miracle.

"Okay," she whispered. "Maybe this won't be so bad after all. Now I need to show you something to balance the scales, right?"

Sabine hesitated and then met Esme's gaze. "Will you… show me how to clean in the human way?"

"What?"

"A bottle broke when I threw the demon," Sabine said, glancing at the cottage again. She would have to find a way to exist among them without losing herself. But not yet.

"Oh, sure," Esme nodded and brushed off her hands. "We brought supplies when we came from the city. I've got a broom and some rags we can use in the cart out front. The whole place needs a good cleaning if we're going to stay here for a while." She absently brushed back a curl. "And no offense, but we need to get you changed into something else. Despite the way the demons were checking you out, a bloody nightgown is *not* a good look."

Sabine blinked. "Are all humans so forthright?"

Esme grinned. "Most of us, yeah."

Sabine frowned, unsure if that was admirable or terrifying.

"Come on," Esme said with a laugh. "I'll show you how to clean up and then we can work on perfecting your human glamour. Your glow is pretty, but definitely not human."

CHAPTER TWELVE

"The nobles likely think you're imprisoned or dead," Balkin said. "If I don't return soon, they'll start a war in your name."

Sabine sat on the edge of the rickety porch, a blanket wrapped around her shoulders. The fabric still smelled faintly of smoke and crushed herbs—Esme's doing, no doubt. Dawn cast gray light across the horizon, staining the clouds in muted colors. The human world was quieter than Faerie. Still. Empty. It unnerved her more than she cared to admit.

Far in the distance, a faint pulse of green shimmered above the trees—fae-wrought light sources, likely a patrol or scouting party. They'd crossed into human lands before, ignoring the boundary lines.

Balkin and Esmelle had cloaked the cottage in wards, but even those couldn't hold forever. The Seelie were still hunting. And if they found her, no border or ward would keep her safe.

"Or they'll think I'm responsible," she murmured, her fingers curling around the blanket's edge. "That I murdered my mother to claim her throne. Why else would I have fled instead of defending my name or seeking vengeance?"

Balkin crouched beside her, his golden eyes gleaming in the soft light. "Those who know you would never believe you responsible. King Cadan'ellesar was seen riding through the forest on the night your mother was killed. The Seelie King's hatred for you and your mother was no secret."

Sabine stared out at the trees around the cottage, recalling the broken image of her mother in the clearing.

"Rhys doesn't know the truth," she whispered. "And I just left him behind."

Balkin took her hand in his furred one. "You must harden your heart, my darling kitten. Your brother is lost to you. He is an agent of the light and will obey his king's will."

A hollow ache formed in her chest, and Sabine pulled her hand away. "I refuse to believe that."

Balkin sighed. "It will likely be several months or even longer before I can return to you. In that time, you must work tirelessly to control your magic and bind the demons to your will."

She turned sharply toward him. "So long?"

"We cannot risk Seelie spies learning your location."

Sabine swallowed hard. She wanted to beg him to stay, to take her with him—anything. But pride prevented the words from falling from her lips. She would not shame her lineage by showing such weakness.

She pulled the blanket closer. "Will you tell the Unseelie nobles I'm alive?"

Balkin shook his head. "Not yet. If they know you live, it will fracture the court. Some will rally to your side, demanding your return. Others will see your absence as an opportunity—to whisper alliances, to test loyalties, and to claim the power you left behind."

"Then let them believe I'm dead for now." Her voice felt brittle in her throat. "At least they won't come looking."

"They *will* look. Rumors are likely already spreading. But if I control the narrative, I can delay what's coming." He lifted his clawed hand as if to touch her and then lowered it with a sigh. "You need time, Sabin'theoria. Time to master your strength and learn who you are away from Faerie and your mother's shadow."

She stiffened beneath the weight of his words.

"Dax and Bane will keep you safe," he added. "In exchange, your Unseelie magic will allow them to thrive outside the underworld."

Sabine squeezed her eyes shut. "If you'd planned all this, how could you not have warned my mother?"

"You think this is what I anticipated?" Balkin demanded with a growl. "Queen Mali'theoria was plotting to take your rightful crown. I knew it was only a matter of time before it was *your* body discovered in the forest. I refused to allow that to happen."

Sabine recoiled as if struck. Her heart stuttered, and for a breathless moment, she couldn't find the ground beneath her. "What?"

Balkin's gaze turned hard. "Years ago, after your magic manifested, I overheard a conversation I was never meant to hear."

He turned to face the trees. His shoulders were taut, tension pulled tight as drawn bowstrings. "Your mother spoke of uniting the courts—Seelie and Unseelie. Not through diplomacy or marriage, like the Council had attempted with your parents. Through domination."

Sabine frowned. "What are you saying, Balkin?"

"She was going to use your magic to become Queen of

both courts," Balkin said flatly. "You were a vessel to her—light and dark in one bloodline. The perfect key to unify Faerie under her rule."

"No," Sabine whispered. "That's not—she wouldn't—"

"She never intended to step aside, kitten." His voice gentled. "She never meant for you to rule. Both your father and mother needed you dead, but for very different reasons."

A knot coiled in her gut, twisting around the memory of her mother's harsh lessons and her father's cold eyes. If what he was saying was true, then everything she'd believed was a lie.

She swallowed. "Will Rhys be safe?"

Balkin's whiskers twitched, the only sign he was troubled by her question. "For now. Your father will keep him close. He'll need to parade his son before the Seelie court to prove stability after what's happened. But safety in Faerie is never simple, kitten. If the Seelie King suspects Rhys'ellesar doubts him, that protection will vanish as quickly as it's given."

"He won't want to see it," she whispered. "He still believes Father can be reasoned with."

"Then hope he never learns otherwise," Balkin said.

Sabine adjusted the blanket around her. "There were… listening crystals in the palace. I found them the night—" Her voice caught, and she shook her head, unable to say the words. "One was hidden in Rhys's room, and another in mine. There may have been more."

Balkin's eyes narrowed. "You're certain?"

Sabine hesitated and then nodded. "I believe so. I left them in place so as not to alert the culprit that they'd been discovered."

"Then Cadan found a way to get past the wards," he murmured. "Only a servant or your mother could have placed them in the royal wing. The rot in the Unseelie court is deeper than I expected. I will have to explore this upon my return."

Sabine brushed her fingers over the locket around her neck. "Did… Did Giannia know about my mother, Balkin?"

"I did not share this information with anyone other than Usagi, and the demons now sworn to protect you. I could not risk anyone discovering my plan. But Giannia…" He sighed. "She loved you well, kitten. She did not trust easily, and her harpy instincts often warned her of the truth that most others would rather ignore. She must have known, or at least suspected."

She lifted her gaze to meet his golden eyes. "Why didn't you tell me all of this sooner?"

"Because I didn't want it to be true," he said quietly. "I thought there would be decades before I'd need to act. I never imagined… that it would begin with blood. That Queen Mali'theoria would—could—fall like this."

Sabine wrapped the blanket tighter, but it did little to ease the chill sinking into her bones. "If my father amassed enough power to kill the strongest Unseelie queen in generations, he'll find me. Two demons and a part-dryad witch won't be enough to stop him."

"No, but this will give us a chance."

"A chance for what?"

"For you to decide what kind of queen you will be." His voice was fierce now. "One who bows to no court. One who forges a new path. It will give you time to find the strength we all have seen blazing within you."

He rose and stepped back, his golden eyes lingering on her like the last flicker of warmth before a fire goes out. "The demons will test you. So will the witch. But they will not break you—unless you let them."

Sabine didn't move, not even when he shifted fully into his lion form and padded toward the edge of the forest.

"Wait," she called softly.

He paused.

"You will come back to me? You swear it?"

Balkin looked back, and through their bond, she felt it. His presence in her thoughts was fierce, protective, and unwavering. And beneath it… full of love and pride.

"Always."

Then he vanished into the trees, and for the first time in her life, Sabine was truly alone.

CHAPTER THIRTEEN

"Focus, little fae," Dax said, circling her like a predator scenting blood. "I can feel it, you know. The way your magic rises and your blood heats when I get close."

Sabine turned with him, heart pounding. Her bare feet scraped against the floor, each breath drawn sharp. The knife in her hand made her movements awkward and clunky, despite the endless days she'd spent training with it.

"You're trying to distract me."

His grin deepened. "You're beautiful when you're angry. And unpredictable magic?" He ran his tongue across his lips. "That's my favorite kind."

She lashed outward, swiping at him with her blade. He slid out of reach, fingers grazing her waist. His movements were like an intimate dance—matching her steps, anticipating her strikes, riding the current of her frustration like a wave.

It was maddening.

He took a step closer, and she barely avoided his grasp.

"Come now, beautiful. I've been waiting to get you under me since the moment I tasted your magic."

Sabine narrowed her eyes, trying to clamp down on the power threatening to rise again. Suppressing her instincts was harder than expected, especially while wielding a mundane weapon and ignoring his taunts.

"Perhaps I'll see if I can undress you before you strike me," Dax said, his heated gaze searing her from within.

Sabine slashed out again with her blade. The infuriating demon darted forward, impossibly fast, and sliced through her blouse with a sharpened claw. The whisper of fabric tearing was louder than any scream.

Sabine's temper snapped.

A blast of raw, searing energy shot through her palm. Dax barely had time to blink before the force hurled him off his feet. He flew backward and crashed through the far wall in a spray of wood, dust, and startled garden herbs.

Something green and leafy fluttered to the ground.

Silence.

Sabine's magic buzzed like lightning in her veins, but her stomach churned.

A furious shout echoed from outside. *"My moonfern!* Do you know how long it takes to grow that?"

Esme burst forward, dirt-streaked and wild-eyed, brandishing a muddy trowel like a blade. "That's it! I've had it. Get out of my garden, Dax. This is a no-demon zone!"

From the garden, Dax laughed, low and amused, "I'm still admiring the view."

Sabine glared at him through the hole in the wall. Turning on her heel, she ripped off the shredded shirt and stomped upstairs. Of all the brainless, childish ways to lose control. At this rate, the demons would be making another trip into the city to buy more clothes tomorrow.

She knew he was taunting her. Testing her.

And yet she kept falling for it.

Every. Single. Time.

Sabine marched back down the stairs, blouse hastily buttoned, anger at her loss of control overriding all her thoughts. She threw open the cottage door and stepped outside into the cool morning air.

Bane sat on the porch sharpening a long, curved blade, his obsidian skin gleaming in the morning light. Without looking up, he asked, "Doing a bit of renovating this morning?"

Sabine shot him a murderous glare.

He held up his blade, studying the sharpened edge. "Should we plan on purchasing materials for a new roof next?"

She bit back the sharp retort on the tip of her tongue. "We were sparring."

"Hmm." His low hum rolled through her like smoke. "Sounded more like foreplay."

She turned back to him and narrowed her eyes, her magic quickly rising. "Careful, demon."

He sheathed the knife with deliberate slowness, the slide of steel against the leather sending goosebumps down her arms. His eyes lifted to hers, full of silent challenge. "Who are you fighting, Sabin'theoria? My brother? Or yourself?"

Sabine paused, then tilted her head to study him, wondering if she was truly that transparent.

Bane stood and prowled toward her, the boards creaking under his weight. His amber gaze pinned her where she stood, as if he could strip away every defense she'd built.

Maybe he could.

He stepped close enough for the air to shift between them. An intense darkness rose upward and surrounded her, not suffocating but all-encompassing. Her breath hitched and she closed her eyes, struggling to control her reaction. Her magic wanted to reach out to him, to respond to his silent demand.

Then, with deliberate gentleness, Bane pressed a finger beneath her chin and tilted her face upward. She opened her eyes to meet his gaze.

"Dax'than tests limits," he murmured. "Find yours, little one."

She searched his expression. "And what about you? Do you test limits as well?"

Bane studied her for a long moment. His expression didn't change, but something darker moved behind his eyes.

"*I* eliminate them."

The words hung between them, sinking beneath her skin like a brand. It wasn't a threat. It was a promise.

Something warned that this demon could be far more dangerous than his brother, yet... she couldn't find it within her to fear him. Something about his power made her think of safety in the darkness. She wanted to explore it, or at least her magic did. Her hands curled into fists as she fought to battle back her instincts.

Bane released her and stepped back, returning to his weapons as if nothing had occurred.

Nonplussed, she stepped off the porch and headed toward the trees. Dry leaves crunched underfoot as she crossed into the woods. Cool air brushed against her over-heated skin. It didn't quell the confusion and frustration warring within her.

It wasn't just the embarrassment at her lack of control, or even Dax's taunting still echoing in her head.

It was her.

She hated how easily she lost control. Hated how much

her magic responded to both of them. She couldn't remember ever struggling so much with the lessons she'd learned back in Faerie, but then again, she'd never had to suppress herself so fully either.

The trees thickened as she moved deeper into the woods. A faint shimmer in the air marked the edge of the warding. She stopped and dropped onto a moss-covered log, her head in her hands. Her chest rose and fell with uneven breaths.

What was she doing here?

Esme's voice rang out, sharp and furious. "Do you have any idea how upset that moonfern is? It's wilting. Wilting! And it's upsetting the rest of the herbs in the garden!"

Sabine didn't lift her head. "I'll reassure it once I get back."

Esme stepped in front of her, bare toes nearly under Sabine's nose. Her foot tapped impatiently.

Sabine lifted her head. Esme's red hair was windblown and wild, and a trace of dirt was smeared across her nose. "You're not the only one who's having trouble adjusting here. Do you think I like being stuck in a cabin with two grumpy demons and an uptight Faerie princess? Get over yourself, Sabin'theoria."

Sabine stared at her.

Esme crossed her arms over her chest. "I was kidnapped by demons. Tossed over a horse's back like luggage. Dragged through the woods. Threatened with all manner of torture. Then they dangle a new shop and your magic in front of my nose, if I'll teach a fae how to play human."

"What?"

"You didn't know?" Esme asked, her brow raised imperiously. "Well, maybe if you'd quit feeling sorry for yourself and actually focus on embracing your new reality, you'll start to see the world a bit differently. Until then, I want you in the garden apologizing to the moonfern. Then, you can figure out how you're going to fix that wall, because I'm *not* sleeping with bugs tonight."

Sabine watched the part-dryad witch storm off, her colorful skirts swishing around her ankles like an angry lion's tail.

Silence returned. A slow wind rustled the trees. Sabine stared at her hands, faint traces of silver light still flickering beneath her skin.

Esme was right.

She hadn't been fully committed.

Her thoughts, her heart—they were still back in Faerie, lingering in the shadows of her mother's death, Giannia's murder, the loss of her brother, and a kingdom she wasn't sure she even wanted.

But she didn't have the luxury of indecision.

If she couldn't master herself, she would never master her magic.

Sabine drew a breath, deeper this time. This wasn't a test. It was a challenge. And maybe, just maybe, she would come out stronger once she'd mastered it.

She just had to stop looking behind her. Find a new way forward.

"This is why I always warn my brothers and sisters to stay away from demons," said a small, high-pitched voice near her shoulder. "They smell like sulfur too. It lingers."

Sabine jerked upright. A blur of shimmering wings darted into view.

A tiny figure hovered midair. A wide smile, delicate wings, a pink dress, and matching hair arranged like flower petals completed the curious vision. The creature gave her a cheerful wave.

"Hi!"

Sabine's mouth dropped open.

With a flick of her wrist, she formed a small bubble around the pixie, capturing her. The pixie's eyes widened. She poked a finger against the bubble's surface, her mouth forming an 'o'. She cocked her head and then licked the edge of the glowing sphere.

"I knew it! Your magic tastes like honeyed sunshine!"

Sabine swallowed, darting a glance back through the trees at the cabin. "How did you find me?"

"I turned left at the oak tree, followed the pollen down by the river, then had a talk with the frog at the pond over the hill, and then…"

Sabine leaned in closer. "How. Did. You. Find. Me?"

The pixie scratched her head, then shrugged. "I followed the yummy magic. It was an added bonus I got to watch you toss a demon through a wall. Ten points for form!"

Sabine frowned, her thoughts racing. Her magic had flared—wild and unguarded. And the pixie had come straight to her. Her pulse quickened as realization struck. Pixies were lesser fae and followed the light… just like the Seelie.

Just like her father.

And now they knew where she was.

Oh, gods. What had she done?

CHAPTER FOURTEEN

"I'm Blossom, by the way."

The pixie hovered in the air, completely unbothered by the glowing sphere holding her captive. If anything, she looked delighted as she spun in a lazy circle, studying Sabine with wide, iridescent eyes that shifted color like the wings of a dragonfly.

Sabine stared at her, then glanced toward the cottage. A pixie. Here. It shouldn't be possible. Not with the wards they'd enabled around the perimeter.

"What happens if I dust it?" the pixie asked, tapping the bubble's edge. She clenched her fists and wiggled her body, sending a smear of glittery dust cascading over the inside of the bubble. "Ooooh! Pretty!"

Sabine frowned. "How did you even manage to sneak through the wards?"

"Wards are for keeping big people out. They're just suggestions for pixies." She cocked her head and added, "Or maybe challenges."

Sabine made a mental note to tell Esme. If pixies could slip through unnoticed, others might too.

Blossom touched the bubble again, finger-painting what appeared to be an extremely unflattering picture of a grumpy demon with her dust. Despite herself, Sabine's lips twitched in a smile.

"It's not very polite to spy."

"I wasn't spying," Blossom protested, twirling in midair. "I was *observing*. There's a difference. And besides, if I *was* spying, I wouldn't have announced myself. That would've been a very bad spy move."

"Why were you observing?"

"I thought you might need help," Blossom said with a shrug. "Demons eat pixies. I wasn't sure if they ate big people too. I was working on an exit strategy in case you needed to escape. But then you looked so sad, and I thought maybe I could cheer you up."

Sabine considered her for a moment. "You weren't sent here to find me? Perhaps by King Cadan'ellesar of the Seelie?"

Blossom's eyes widened. "He's even worse than the demons!"

Sabine arched her brow. "Oh?"

"He pinches wings," Blossom whispered, as if revealing a grave crime. "Just pinches them. Right at the base where it hurts most. One time, my third cousin's aunt's brother sneezed in a garden when the Seelie King was nearby, and he almost twisted his wings clear off!"

Her wings turned red and she sniffled. "He never flew right again."

Sabine lifted her hands to cradle the bubble, wanting to soothe the pixie's distress. "I didn't realize King Cadan'ellesar was so cruel to you."

Blossom sniffed and nodded. "That's why my family left the Seelie court. My parents didn't want to risk anything like that happening to me or my brothers and sisters.

We've been living in and around the Silver Forest since then."

Sabine released the bubble with a flick of her fingers. The sphere unraveled into strands of magic and vanished.

She sent a light wave of magic over the pixie, watching as her wings turned back to their normal, shimmery iridescence. Blossom trilled happily and beamed a smile up at her.

"What's your name?"

Sabine smiled down at her and asked, "Can I trust you?"

Blossom nodded eagerly.

She leaned down and whispered, "Sabin'theoria."

"The missing Faerie princess," Blossom breathed, her wings twitching excitedly. "My brother, Barley, once drank from a flower you touched outside the Winter Palace. He said it tasted like sunlight and starberries. And now you're here! Right in front of me! And I'm... TOUCHING YOU!!!"

Blossom squealed and jumped up and down on her palm. "It's me! I'm touching her! She magicked me!"

The pixie dove down and hugged Sabine's thumb. "You need a pixie sidekick, don't you? Someone to help you wrangle demons, right? We can be the unstoppable duo! Magic and mischief! Sparkles and doom!"

Sabine laughed, but it faded a moment later as she realized it had been the first time in weeks that she'd truly smiled, much less laughed. And somehow, the tiny creature in front of her had made it feel almost easy. Something in Sabine's heart lightened at the realization.

"I'm not sure how well my demon companions would enjoy having a pixie around."

Blossom cocked her head, considering it. "You know, I could be a lot of help to you. I hear things. Important things!"

"Spying again?"

"Still observing," Blossom said sagely. "And I didn't even *try* to hear anything. Sometimes the dandelions tell me things. Especially the older ones. They hold onto memories if the words are strong enough. Only pixies know how to listen properly."

She reached into the folds of her dress, which seemed to function as a pouch, and pulled out a slightly squashed dandelion puff. Its golden stem had dried to a pale thread, but most of the seeds still clung to it like a crown of tiny stars.

"I found this one yesterday outside your window. It liked listening," Blossom said. "I asked it to share with me."

Sabine's brow furrowed. "Share what?"

Blossom blew a sharp breath across the seeds, and they swirled around Sabine in a sparkling spiral. Magic tickled against her skin, gentle as breath and sharp as memory.

A man's voice emerged from the air. *"Every time I feel her magic or get my hands on her, this insatiable hunger rises up. Fuck, the thought of being bonded directly to her... Imagine that kind of power moaning your name. Tell me you wouldn't be tempted."*

A second voice followed, deeper, colder. *"Her beastman will kill you."*

"Heh. Some things might be worth dying for."

Sabine's breath hitched, her face warming from the heat in the overheard words.

The dandelion seeds scattered like ash, vanishing into the air. She stared down at the empty stem in Blossom's hand. "Those were Dax and Bane's voices."

She didn't know what disturbed her more—the overheard desire, the thought of a bond with a demon, or the fact that a pixie had just handed her an unfiltered truth she wasn't meant to hear.

Blossom nodded, wobbling slightly in midair. "Takes a lotta magic," she murmured and then blinked, as if remembering something. "Oh! That's not all I've heard."

Sabine held out her hand for the pixie to land. "What else?"

"Before we left the Seelie Palace, my brother overheard King Cadan'ellesar talking to his dreamweavers…"

Sabine stilled. "Oh?"

Blossom glanced around and leaned closer. "They've been manipulating dreams. One of the Councilors said he could get close enough to the Unseelie to dose their wine and make them susceptible to the dreamweavers. Then they can slip into anyone's mind while they sleep. Move people around like game pieces."

Sabine sank onto the log, her knees suddenly weak. Usagi had warned her, asking if she remembered her dreams. Was this what she'd meant?

"What else?" she asked quietly.

Blossom shrugged. "I'm not sure. They mentioned crystals and spying. Barley wasn't sure if they were talking about *him* spying, so he flew out of the garden before they could spot him." She tilted her head thoughtfully. "Maybe it's good you're not in Faerie anymore. It doesn't sound like that wine would taste very good."

Sabine stared at the tiny creature, her heart pounding. Dreamweavers. Crystals. Cadan's reach ran deeper than she'd feared. He'd turned their loyal servants into puppets.

Giannia's face flashed through her mind, and Sabine touched the locket around her neck. It could have even been Giannia who planted the listening crystal. Not by choice, but because someone had stolen her will through dreams.

All the blood drained from her face as another possibility struck her.

What if *she* had been the one to plant the listening crystals? Could her father have manipulated her or Rhys into taking such action?

A wave of nausea rose up quickly. She was no threat to him. Neither was Rhys. He had to know that.

Blossom let out a tiny yawn, her wings drooping. Sabine absently sent a soft wave of fortifying power over the pixie, making her trill happily in response.

People all her life had kept secrets from her, making decisions on her behalf because they thought they knew better. And those same people could easily be manipulated if the wrong person pulled the strings.

If Balkin had confided in her, perhaps things would have turned out differently. At least she would have been more cautious. Maybe even Giannia and her mother would have—

Sabine took a shaky breath. The time for regrets was gone.

If she was going to be queen in truth, she needed to stop relying on other people to make decisions for her.

And for that… she needed information.

Blossom held out the dandelion stem like it was a trophy. "See? I'm very good at secrets. And also very good at delivering them." She paused. "I like the witch. The plants like her too. She sings to her tea leaves. That's always a good sign."

Sabine exhaled slowly and took the stem. She twirled it in her fingers and said, "I don't know what to make of you. Or if I can truly trust you."

"You will," Blossom said with a smile. "I have a really good feeling about this."

Sabine gave a soft laugh. "Fine. You can stay. But you need to make sure the demons don't see you."

Blossom nodded eagerly. "And the witch?"

Sabine's eyes drifted toward the cottage again. She liked Esme, far more than she'd expected. But her life in Faerie had taught her the dangers about trusting too soon. "For now, let's keep our partnership just between us. Maybe we can include her in the future."

"Got it," Blossom said, beaming. "You'll hardly notice I'm there."

Sabine highly doubted that. But somehow, she didn't mind the idea—though a small part of her wondered if anything born of Faerie ever arrived by accident.

CHAPTER FIFTEEN

Sabine woke to the scent of flowers and the lingering memory of the Winter Palace gardens, but the illusion shattered when she opened her eyes to the cracks running across the loft's ceiling beams. She frowned up at them.

If the tree were still alive, it would have been embarrassed to have its rings showing in such an unseemly fashion.

Sunlight spilled through the loft window, casting a harsh light on the worn floorboards near her bed. She kicked off the scratchy blanket and glanced at the empty cot beside her.

Esme was already gone, likely tending the garden. Ever since Sabine had shown her how to coax plants into responding to her touch, the part-dryad witch had spent nearly every waking hour in the dirt.

Sabine yawned and stretched, marveling at how centered she felt despite her surroundings. For the first time in days, her body didn't feel like it was tearing itself in two. The dull war between light and shadow, that constant pull of opposing forces within her, had somehow quieted.

As she sat up, a cascade of colorful flowers tumbled into her lap. She blinked and picked one up, inhaling its sweet fragrance. With a frown, she reached up to find a dozen more woven into a braided crown that hadn't been there when she fell asleep.

Blossom.

"Could it be so simple?" she murmured, brushing her thumb over a soft petal.

The demons spoke to her Unseelie side. They grounded her. Kept her tethered. But something else had bloomed within her after meeting the pixie. Something lighter. Wilder. She'd laughed for the first time. It had become easier to smile.

Maybe it was the flowers. Or the pixie magic still clinging to her skin and hair.

Whatever it was, it had left her more whole than she'd felt since leaving Faerie.

She ran her fingers over her braids, carefully pulling out the flowers one by one and tucking them safely beneath her blanket. The last thing she needed was for one of the demons to ask why she was hoarding wildflowers— or to discover the tiny pixie who would make an excellent appetizer.

She left the braids alone. Their presence was... comforting, in a strange sort of way. And would, hopefully, keep her hair out of the way during today's training session.

A faint rustle near the window caught her attention. Blossom sat on the windowsill, her legs swinging back and forth as if she hadn't a care in the world.

Sabine arched a brow and gestured to her braids. Playing in her hair while Sabine slept had likely fortified the pixie far beyond her normal limits. That was partly why they weren't usually allowed inside the palace walls. Pixies had a great propensity for mischief, and the close proximity to that much magic usually turned their small shenanigans into epic-sized ones.

"You've been busy this morning."

Blossom grinned. "Your magic's even better than caffeinated nectar. I don't think I slept more than two hours!"

"You need to be careful," she warned. "Dax and Bane are probably downstairs. You do realize they'll eat you if they catch you, right?"

Blossom squeaked and flew over to press her tiny hand against Sabine's lips. "Don't even put that out in the universe!" When Sabine held out her hand, Blossom landed and said, "They're down at the clearing, growling at each other over who gets to train with you this morning. I think Dax is winning the argument, and Bane's going to take over this afternoon."

Sabine sighed. Dax was always inventive when trying to fracture her control, while Bane tended to be a harsher taskmaster. "This should be interesting."

Blossom tilted her head, considering it. "I think you can take them. Especially if I go spy—er, *observe*. Yeah. Observe their plans and report back to you."

Without another word, Blossom's image shimmered into that of a ladybug, and she zipped out the window.

Sabine bit back a smile and turned to the tarnished mirror. Something softened within her at the sight of the braided crown. Even wearing the human glamour they'd settled on didn't bother her as much.

She leaned closer, studying her reflection. Her glow was still tamped down, her features… flatter. Her hair looked more blondish white than true silver, and her eyes were a pale blue instead of lavender. She hadn't slipped, even while sleeping. The ears were still pointed, but rounding them hurt. Esme had assured her there were enough mixed bloodlines in Akros that pointed ears wouldn't raise eyebrows.

Sabine pulled out a sleeveless dark-green tunic and soft black pants. Blossom's words echoed through her thoughts, and she narrowed her eyes as a plan took shape.

She exchanged the pants for another pair, one that hugged her curves more tightly, and tugged them into place. Then she unbuttoned the top of her blouse. "Challenge *my* control, huh?"

After a second thought, she opened the next two buttons, exposing more than a hint of cleavage.

"We'll see about that."

She cinched the tunic with a leather sash, fastened the arm guards Bane had purchased for her two days ago, and slid the knife into the sheath at her hip. A second, smaller blade found its home at the small of her back.

With a small, satisfied smile, she turned and headed downstairs. Outside, the morning sunlight warmed her face, and she lifted her nose to the breeze, catching a faint trace of the sea and salt on the wind.

She'd never seen the ocean, though Bane's stories of the nearby human city had filled her with restless curiosity.

Akros.

The name floated through her mind like a warning. It was once a city devoted to the ancient gods, worshipped before they abandoned this world. Now, it served as a haven for the human refugees who had become trapped on Aeslion after the portal was sealed.

She shook her head, pushing aside her unease. She'd deal with that reality later. For now, she had to embrace her plan and prove to the demons once and for all that she wasn't to be trifled with. Straightening her shoulders, she headed toward the clearing behind the house where a makeshift practice ring had been set up.

The demons circled like predators, sunlight glinting off their blades and the taut lines of their bodies. This wasn't playful sparring. They were masters of their arts, pitting their wills against one another. They moved with real weapons and a kind of ferocity that sent a silent thrill through her.

She swallowed.

Gods. Maybe this plan was a terrible idea.

As if they sensed her approach, they both turned toward her. Sabine let a small smile play about her lips and walked toward them, putting a slight swing into her steps. Dax's eyes heated as he perused her up and down.

Bane studied her, his expression immediately suspicious. "You're... looking different this morning."

Her smile deepened as she stepped into the training circle. She absently trailed her fingers across Bane's chest as she walked by him, causing his eyes to flash silver. "Which one of you do I get to play with first?"

Dax took a step forward, his lips curving upward. "Careful, Princess. If it's play you want, I can give you the kind you'll remember. You'll be far too busy to even consider dancing with my brother."

He reached for her wrist as if to pull her close. She drew her dagger and quickly sidestepped in one smooth motion. As she pressed it against his gut, she leaned in close and whispered next to his ear, "Promises, promises."

Dax's eyes flared silver, sending a dark thrill through her. Magic simmered under her skin, but she kept it in check and moved away from him. He darted toward her again, but she was ready.

Sabine twisted, letting his momentum carry him past.

She caught his arm and pivoted hard, sending him sprawling into the dirt with a satisfying thud.

With a growl, he leaped up and dove toward her.

Sabine ducked low, aiming to sweep his legs, but he anticipated it this time. He caught her mid-motion, one arm hooking around her waist as he twisted, using his greater strength to bring her crashing to the ground.

The impact knocked the air from her lungs. She rolled, trying to escape, but Dax pinned her effortlessly, his knee pressing against her thigh, one hand braced beside her head and capturing her weapon hand. Panic flailed briefly, but she tamped it down.

His face hovered inches from hers, his breath warm against her ear. "You know what they say about demons, don't you? When they finally capture their prey?"

His free hand slid downward, searing her skin like a brand. His thumb traced lightly along the side of her breast before continuing lower to her hip.

Sabine's breath hitched, desire pulsing through her as her magic stirred.

No.

She wouldn't surrender.

She needed to own this—own *him*.

Hooking her leg over him, she slid her hand behind her back as she nipped his earlobe hard enough to draw blood. Dax groaned, his growing hardness pressing against her core. To nearly everyone else, demonic blood was among the strongest of poisons, capable of even taking down greater dragons.

Except she was the Unseelie heir, and darkness thrummed within her as easily as the light.

"Are you planning on teaching me another lesson, Dax?" she purred.

"Fuck, you're potent," he muttered, his gaze lowering to her lips.

Her hand inched lower, fingers curling around the hilt of the hidden blade pressed against her back. As his head dipped toward hers as if to kiss her, she twisted her hips and brought the blade up between them—stopping just shy of his throat.

Dax froze, his silvered eyes gazing at her with undeniable hunger.

Her lips curved in a teasing smile. "You have no idea how potent I can be, Dax. Perhaps you'll find out one day. But it won't be today."

She pressed the blade a fraction closer, just enough to let him feel the truth behind her words.

For a heartbeat, neither of them moved. His weight pinned her, his heat radiating through the thin fabric of her tunic, but the balance had shifted. He knew it. So did she.

And they both relished the challenge the other offered.

Dax eased back with deliberate slowness, his body sliding against hers with an intimacy that wasn't his to claim—yet. He rose to his feet and continued watching her, his fingers twitching as though still memorizing the feel of her.

Sabine stood and resheathed her knives, turning to face Bane. He'd watched the exchange in silence, and now there was something in his eyes she couldn't quite name. He jerked his head toward his brother. "The wards need to be checked."

Dax's hungry gaze roamed over her figure, and he took a step toward her. "Fuck the wards. I'm busy."

Bane's hand shot out and grabbed Dax's shoulder. Before Dax could so much as snarl, Bane leaned in and spoke sharply in the guttural cadence of the demonic tongue.

Sabine watched them, unable to understand the words. But the meaning was clear enough in the tension that snapped between them.

Dax answered with a curse, then tore his gaze from her.

As he stalked toward the forest, Bane started toward her. She remained still and kept her gaze fixed on him, refusing to show any weakness.

He stopped in front of her and searched her expression. After a moment, he raised his clawed hand and gently tilted her chin up.

"For the first time since you arrived, I saw an Unseelie queen step onto the field. Fierce. Deadly. A sight to behold. Hold tight to her, Sabin'theoria. That's not an illusion. It's your truth."

Sabine swallowed as he released her and prowled away. Her skin tingled where he'd touched her, but the approval in his words warmed her in a way she'd never thought possible.

Not an illusion. Your truth.

The words bit deep. She'd lived inside so many illusions, some her own, others forced upon her. But this moment? This strength? This was hers.

She'd bested Dax, not with magic—but with her inner strength and will. Bane recognized that, even if Dax hadn't yet.

The thought sent a surge of giddy emotion through her. She could do this. She *would* do this.

She turned toward the treeline where Dax had vanished, then glanced down at her hands. They no longer trembled.

Reaching for Giannia's locket around her neck, she

unclasped it. The silver metal was cool against her skin, dulled from centuries of wear but still whole.

Running her thumb over the edge of the locket, she thought about that night and Giannia's whispered words. Her tutor had seen something within her, the same way Bane had. They'd both given her an opportunity to truly find herself, even if that meant temporarily hiding the truth in layered illusions.

She walked into the trees, past the edge of the clearing, until she found a quiet patch of damp earth nestled beneath several trees. Kneeling, she dug into the earth with her bare hands, the scent of soil rising around her.

When the hole was deep enough, she lowered the locket into it. Her fingers hovered for a moment, reluctant.

"May you find peace in the Beyond," she whispered.

Then she closed the earth over it and pressed her palm to the dirt. Her magic pulsed, sinking into the ground. A single green shoot burst from the soil, twisting upward, its leaves unfurling as though lazily stretching.

Sabine reached into her pocket and pulled out the small owl figurine Usagi had given her. She cradled it for a moment, then nestled it in the crook of the young tree's roots.

"Watch over what was," she said softly. "I'll become what must be."

The leaves shivered as if in reply.

She stood, brushing the dirt from her hands.

And as she turned away, she left the frightened girl behind in the forest and embraced the queen she was destined to become.

CHAPTER SIXTEEN

~ MALEK ~

Tarvei reeked of salt and smoke.

Malek stood at the edge of the harbor, the clamor of fish merchants and the clang of bells from the eastward tower competing to drown out the low voice of the dockmaster's assistant.

"Magical trinkets, eh? Might have better luck in a place like Akros," the man said with a shrug.

"It's a port town?" Malek asked, glancing at his map. His gaze drifted toward the heavily wooded region beyond the city, where Faerie was rumored to be hidden behind protective barriers.

Not yet.

Breaking the treaty would be a last resort.

"Aye," the assistant said, spitting a dark glob into a copper basin at his feet.

Malek eyed the foul-smelling black smear. Primitive, but effective. Northern sailors mixed pitchroot saliva into a sap that sealed hulls tight enough to withstand even merfolk acid.

Turning back to the map, Malek tapped a finger on the

city name he'd mentioned. "Akros," he said. "I'll see what I can find there."

The assistant snorted. "You won't be sailing to Akros anytime soon. Not without an invite."

Malek narrowed his eyes. "Explain."

Instead of answering, the assistant stroked his long, white beard and arched his brow expectantly. Malek held his gaze for a moment before dropping a handful of coins on the counter. Nothing was free, not even information. He should have known better.

The man grinned wide, his teeth stained black from the pitchroot. "That there be the home of the Thieves' Guild. They control who comes into their city—and who's allowed to leave. You won't be gettin' anywhere near it."

"I find it hard to believe a band of cutthroats control the entire city."

He shrugged, then spat again. "To catch the guild's eye, you need an invite or specialty wares that usually come from... less-than-honest means. Otherwise, you'll be findin' your ship sunk and your crew floatin' in the harbor."

Catching sight of his friend, Levin, weaving through the crowd, Malek rolled up his map. "I see. And how would someone go about securing an invite?"

The assistant's gaze drifted to the modest transport vessel Malek had arrived on. "Prove you're a captain of means first. Then, if you've got the right wares and quite a bit more coin to secure an invitation, I might know someone who knows someone."

Malek gave him a curt nod and dropped the coin pouch on the table. The man snatched it up with greedy fingers.

Turning away, he joined Levin at the edge of the dock. "What did you find out?"

Levin's expression was grim. "Three families claim to

be descended from fae bloodlines. One lied. The other two are too diluted for our purposes. They didn't even register my ring was made of iron when we shook hands."

Malek's jaw clenched. "Then we keep looking."

"Any luck on your end?"

He glanced over his shoulder at the dockmaster's assistant, now deep in a loud argument over repair costs. "Possibly. How do you feel about smuggling?"

Levin cocked his head. "Not the most dangerous thing we've ever done. Might be fun."

Malek grinned and clapped him on the shoulder. "I think we need to consider a new vocation, my friend. Sailing the seas, collecting shiny baubles…"

"And magical artifacts?" Levin asked, chuckling.

"Mmhmm," Malek agreed. "A certain select group of artifacts. But I wouldn't be opposed to hoarding a few other treasures along the way."

A flash of light over the distant treeline caught his eye. He straightened, focusing on the dense forest beyond the city—where the heart of Faerie supposedly lay.

Levin frowned. "What in the name of the underworld is that?"

A flicker of green fire shimmered along the horizon. It wasn't natural. Not even stormlight burned that color.

Even from this distance, it called to something deep within him. Malek stared, his instincts warning the light was important. Dangerous. The urge to hunt surged through him.

Levin grabbed his arm. "Easy, brother. Too many innocents around."

Malek scowled, but Levin's words had broken the spell. "Did you feel that?"

Levin studied him. "No. I saw the light. What was it?"

Malek didn't answer.

For a moment, he'd felt—something. Fleeting, but unmistakable. A delicate wisp of magic had called out to him, fragile as starlight and as alluring as a siren's song.

He forced himself to look away. They were too close to Faerie and his endgame to risk losing control.

His fingers tightened around the map. Every fruitless lead, every diluted bloodline... each one pushed them closer to a future he refused to accept.

Rumors claimed the fae hadn't left their realm in years, but he refused to believe that. Somewhere. Somehow. He'd find what he was looking for.

Perhaps Akros held the key.

ALSO BY JAMIE A. WATERS

THE OMNI TOWERS
(Dystopian Fantasy Romance)

Beneath the Fallen City

Shadow of the Coalition

Tremors of the Past

Drop of Hope

Flames of Redemption

Spirit of the Towers

Ruins of Fate

ABOUT THE AUTHOR

Jamie A. Waters is an award-winning fantasy romance author and dragon enthusiast. Weaving together magic, intrigue, and some delicious romance, she creates memorable and immersive worlds that provide the perfect escape. Her books features strong, capable heroines and their swoon-worthy heroes who will stop at nothing to save the day.

Jamie currently resides in Florida with two neurotic dogs who enjoy stealing socks. When she's not pursuing her passion of writing, she's usually trying to learn new and interesting random things (like how to pick locks or use the self-cleaning feature of the oven without setting off the fire alarm). In her downtime, she enjoys reading on her Kindle, playing computer games, painting, or acting as a referee between the dragons and fairies currently at war inside her closet.

Learn more at: jamieawaters.com.

www.ingramcontent.com/pod-product-compliance
Lightning Source LLC
Chambersburg PA
CBHW021733190726
48288CB00009B/3027